A NOVEL

NOBLE DEEDS

A NOVEL

NOBLE DEEDS

J.J. ZERR

PRIMIX PUBLISHING
THE WRITE CHOICE

Primix Publishing
11620 Wilshire Blvd
Suite 900, West Wilshire Center, Los Angeles, CA, 90025
www.primixpublishing.com
Phone: 1-800-538-5788

Published by Primix Publishing 10/05/2021

ISBN: 978-1-955177-42-9(sc)
ISBN: 978-1-955177-43-6(hc)
ISBN: 978-1-955177-44-3(e)

Library of Congress Control Number: 2021920714

CONTENTS

THE SINS OF THE SON

...THEN IT HIT THE FAN

THE SINS OF THE FATHER

To Sister Mathews

To the Colleens, the Clean Harrys, and the Fireball Freddies.

To a noble breed: sailors and the families they come from.

To the future: the class of 2016.

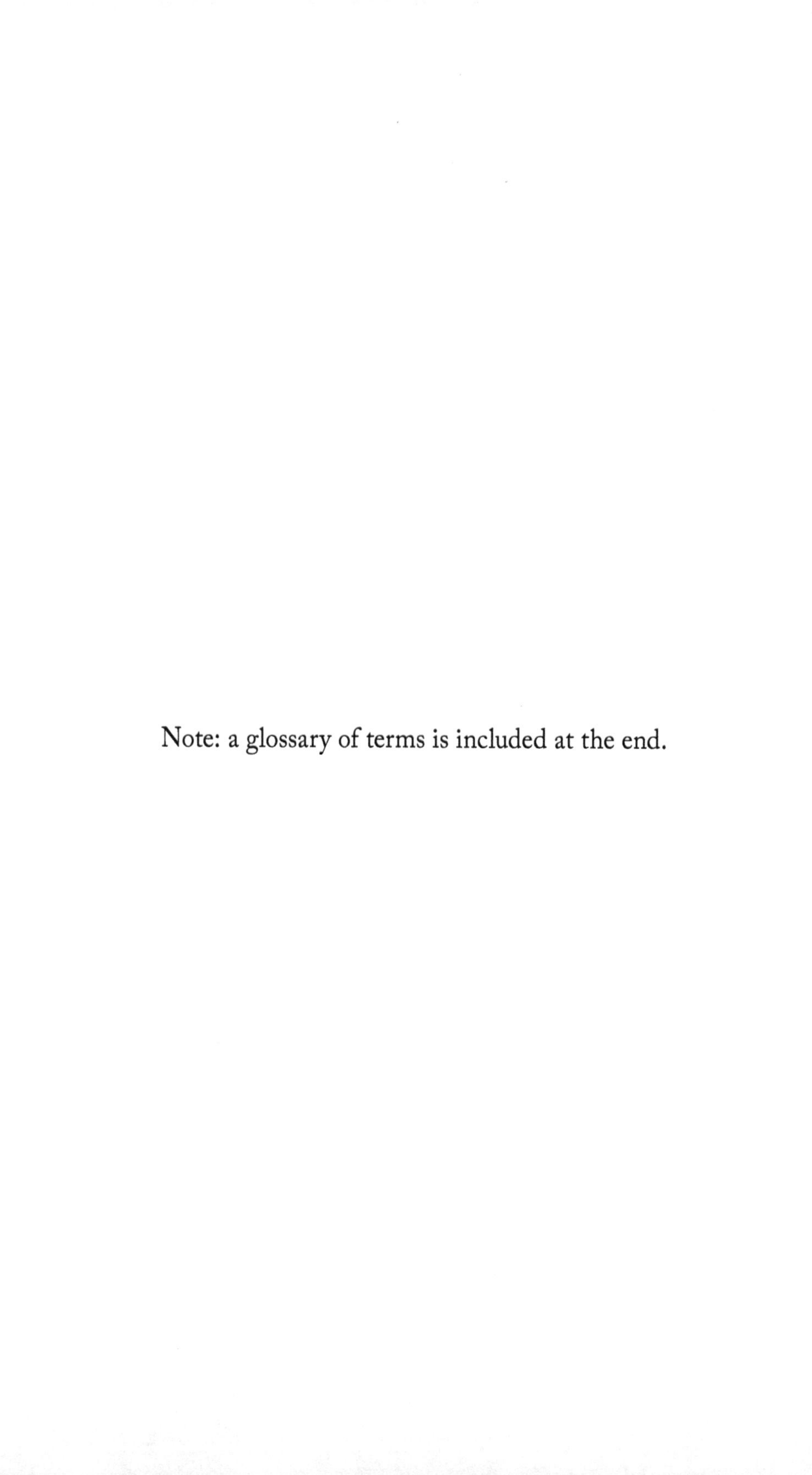

Note: a glossary of terms is included at the end.

I

THE SINS OF THE SON

1

CAPTAIN PETE ADLER

THE SIGN BOLTED TO A steel fencepost in a bucket of cement reserved the parking spot. The sign read, "CO." Captain Pete Adler pulled into the space as if he owned it, which he did. That spot belonged to the commanding officer of the USS *Marianas,* one of the navy's aircraft carriers.

Niggling at the corner of his mind, trying to get in, was the thought that the job was as temporary as a reserved parking spot marked by a portable sign. That thought might get in another time. Not today. Today, Captain Pete Adler was taking *his* carrier to sea for the first time.

Colleen rode with him to the ship. Pete could have had his marine orderly pick him up, but she wanted to ride along. The day was special to her too. Special enough to get her out of bed well before the sun came up. She didn't even groan when the alarm went off.

Pete shoved the gearshift lever of the Chevy van into park and peered out the windshield at the illuminated steel structure looming fifty feet above the pier. He turned his gaze to the flight deck and then the island and the top of the mast sticking up another one hundred fifty feet, pointing to the stars.

He took her hand. She sat in shadow, but he didn't have to see her face to know it radiated love that was as fresh as a newborn's lusty yowl, yet still glowed golden from twenty-five years of marriage and thirty of going steady.

"Have I told you lately that I love you…" she started singing, a song she adored from a fifties Elvis album.

Colleen. That woman could reach a hand inside his chest and fondle his heart, and it *thump, thump, thumped*, happy as a petted dog's tail.

He'd never had a main squeeze. Colleen had been his one and only squeeze since senior year of high school.

"Stop that caterwauling, woman. What will the guys on the quarterdeck think if I walk aboard crying, snot trickling out of my nose and into my mouth?"

"I do love you, Pete Adler."

He leaned over to kiss her. She stuck her tongue in his mouth.

After a moment, he pulled back. "Rats. Now I have to go home and take a cold shower."

Joking was better than saying that he knew he could never make her as happy as she made him. That was the most god-awful thing.

Pete got out. Colleen slipped into the driver's seat. They'd bought the van twelve years before. Pete was going through test pilot school when the fifth daughter was born. The only seat left for baby Molly in their two-door Impala was her mother's lap. The older girls loved the van. They no longer had to be scrunched together with annoying sisters. Colleen appreciated the ability to be able to move from her seat to the back to quell mutinies or to tend to Molly.

Pete watched her click her seat belt, move her purse to the floor beside her, and adjust the rearview mirror. He felt the familiar magnetic pull of the ship tugging him toward his greatest naval adventure. Much of him was anxious to get on the ship, on *his* ship. At the same time, there was a fishhook embedded in his heart. Colleen held the line to the hook, and she tugged at it. Departing for a stint at sea had always contained these two disparate forces drawing and tearing at him.

"Takeoff checklist complete?" Pete asked. "Complete."

Pete kissed her hand and stood looking up at her shadowed face.

"Pete Adler, do I have to remind ye, then, the crew of the mighty warship USS *Marianas,* they be waiting for the commanding officer himself to be coming aboard to take them out upon the briny deep? Be on with ye then."

"Aye, Mrs. Commanding Officer."

Pete saluted her and closed the door, shutting off the overhead light of the van and hiding Colleen in darkness.

2

COMMANDER HAROLD PENNINGTON III

THE EXECUTIVE OFFICER OF THE USS *Marianas*, Com- mander Pennington, stood in the shadow of the island on the flight deck and watched the CO get out of his van and walk toward the brow. The handheld radio crackled static.

"This is the officer of the deck, XO. Cap'n's coming aboard."

The exec double-clicked the mic on his radio to acknowledge the message.

It would have been nice if the CO had scheduled the orderly to pick him up. Then everybody would have known what time the CO was arriving. But COs didn't conduct themselves to make life easier for an XO. It worked the other way.

It was the second time the navy had put him together with Pete. The first time, Harry was CO of one of the F-18 squadrons in Airwing 21. Captain Peter Adler commanded the airwing. The two of them had hit it off. Both had an eye and impatience for BS, bureaucratic *shinola*, Pete called it. Both were Good Sticks. Navy pilots characterized the guys who got the best scores on the bombing ranges, won the mock dogfights, and who knocked down the best carrier landing grades as Good Sticks. No one ever said, "Pete or Harry is a Good Stick." Those who needed to know just knew.

Harry admired Pete because of his experience. Two tours to Vietnam topped his list of reasons. One night in the O Club at Naval Air Station, Lemoore, California, they discovered that they'd both prayed the same prayer in the late sixties and early seventies: "Please, God, don't let the war end before I get there." Pete's prayer had been answered with 330 combat missions. Harry got his wings in 1973 after the first planeloads of POWs had landed in the Philippines. He had missed Nam but fought other kinds of battles in the Pentagon and Naval War College. He had logged enough operational experience to earn an orderly progression through the ranks.

Pete admired Harry for his lack of experience, or so it seemed. Harry smiled, recalling the fitness report he'd received when he detached from the airwing. Captain Adler had written:

> Experience, in terms of flight hours, carrier landings, and combat missions tells something about a man. Everybody needs some experience. Some men, like Commander Pennington, don't need much at all to demonstrate that here is a Good Stick, here is a leader, here is a man who can handle whatever challenges the navy wants to throw at him. Here is a man who will be an admiral.

Harry was six two and burly. His nickname had been Bear. Former Bear watched the "little shit," five-foot-seven Pete, stride across the lighted ramp to the brow. Navy officers—superiors, peers, and some subordinates—referred to Pete that way quite often.

But for an XO, even thinking it was sacrilege—worse, mutiny.

When Pete assumed command of the *Marianas,* he made it clear he wanted a clean ship. Crewmen tracked grease and oil from the flight deck. Feeding five thousand men three times a day, another source of defilement. "Cleaning passageways once a day won't keep up with the mess," he'd said. "But, XO, the cleaning guys can't close off the passageways. I want things clean, but people still have to move forward and aft. Figure out how to do it." The CO wanted a clean ship another way too. Pete hated drugs and especially hated the idea of drugs on his ship.

A week after taking over, Pete addressed the crew on the flight deck, laying out the things he expected of "all of us *Marianas* sailors…"

The XO shook his head. In a week, Pete had the crew eating out of his hand. He had that way of making himself one of the thousands, while at the same time, clearly establishing himself as the alpha, the high-hooba-jooba bubba, the boss, the commanding *friggin'* officer. During that talk, he'd dropped the Clean Harry nickname on his exec. It spread. And stuck.

The little shit was something.

3

COLLEEN

SHE WATCHED PETE CLIMB THE ladder and cross the brow to the quarterdeck.

You've come a long way for a Missouri farm boy, Pete Adler.

Colleen remembered when Pete had gotten the call. She left the sink, dried her hands, and picked up the kitchen phone.

He was at the table helping Eileen with seventh-grade math. According to Pete, Eileen's brain rejected algebra like a body rejected a donor organ with an incompatible blood type. Still, he was so patient with her. She fretted, fussed, fumed, and he never raised his voice, just calmly tried to find another way to explain a concept.

"For you," Colleen said, and then she handed him the phone. Something the caller said surprised Pete. He listened and then said, "Thank you, sir," and hung up. He kept his hand on the wall phone.

The way Pete acted, it must have been bad news. Then he turned, and shook his head. *Bad, but what?* she wondered.

He just stood there, frowning. "Pete?"

A grin bloomed over his face. He pumped his arms and his feet stomped up and down. He seemed to want to scream.

"Pete, what is it?"

He stopped dancing, looked her in the eye, still grinning. "A carrier," he said. "I screened for an aircraft carrier."

He started laughing.

She remembered thinking about that word *screened* and felt as if she understood it for the first time. When the navy selected a man to command a squadron of planes or a ship, he *screened* for command. The screening process was like dumping a large number of people onto a fine-meshed sieve. Most got segregated and dumped aside with the chaff and tare.

"A friggle-frappin' aircraft carrier!" he said.

"Hey! How about my friggle-frapping algebra?" Eileen asked.

Colleen and Pete were both stunned. It took them a moment to understand that Eileen really hadn't said naughty words.

Simultaneously, laughter exploded from both of them. They pulled Eileen to her feet and the trio stumbled in a clumsy dance around the kitchen.

That night had been the finest the navy had ever allowed them. So many times, they'd sweated new assignments and promotion lists. But after the call, all their anxiety over the future, whether they had one or not, all went away.

An aircraft carrier!

And Eileen's friggle-frapping math. Pete said once, "The only thing that has been like Eileen encountering puberty was Chernobyl."

Eileen was a handful.

Pete had disappeared inside the ship. "Oh hear us when we cry to Thee, For those in peril on the sea," she prayed aloud. It was her prayer every time Pete went to sea.

Peril. In many ways, that's what an aircraft carrier was: a floating steel box of peril. Aircraft accident rates were several times higher for navy carrier pilots than for air force counterparts. Just moving the planes around the flight deck, with inches to spare between wing tips, was hazardous. And the bombs. Pete had lost a cousin, one of 134 killed, in the *Forrestal* fire off Vietnam. The cousin was from his mother's family, the ones they never visited. Still, a relative, cousin Del.

The *Forrestal*'s flight deck video camera recorded Del's death. Pete had seen the film. In the movie, a tall skinny kid, Del, manned a fire hose by himself. He aimed the stream at a bomb hung from an airplane wing rack. Beneath the bomb was a puddle of burning jet fuel. There was a flash. When the whiteout materialized into a picture again, the plane was gone, just a view of ocean. Del, gone too.

Pete only talked about Del once, but Colleen knew he often thought about his vaporized cousin from the estranged side of his family.

She started the engine to drive home, which was Quarters J across from the O Club, where the girls slept like angels. Sleeping, even Eileen qualified.

"For those in peril on the sea."

She backed out of Pete's parking spot. "Amen," she said.

4

CAPTAIN PETE ADLER

It was early. The ship wasn't getting under way until 0930, but Pete wanted a bit of that morning for himself. Arriving at 0445 didn't ensure solitude, but the chances were decent.

The CO's in-port cabin was on the 03 level, just across the passageway from Admiral Miller's quarters. Miller was a battle group commander, and *Marianas* served as his flagship. He wouldn't be aboard that week. The ship was providing carrier landing services to A-7 and F-14 training squadrons. The next time the ship went to sea, other ships of the group would sail with the carrier. Miller would be aboard then, commanding his battle group.

Pete didn't enter his cabin. What he wanted, or maybe needed, to do was to visit with the previous commanding officers of the *Marianas.* Their framed photos hung in a row tacked to the bulkhead in the passageway outside the door to his room. All nineteen men were still alive, but Pete thought each of them had left a wisp of soul behind when they turned over command. When he looked at the photos, and no one else was around, he felt their spiritual presence. He felt something else that morning. The past COs expected him to take damn good care of their aircraft carrier.

He saluted them. Then he climbed four ladders to his at-sea cabin, located just aft of the pilothouse. He stashed his toiletries and skivvies and noted that the steward had brought his cassette player up from below. Neil Diamond and Johnny Cash to shave to. Chopin's nocturnes and Liszt's symphonies for the end of the day.

He walked out to the bridge.

Good, no one here.

Soon the pilothouse would fill up with phone talkers, bearing shooters, lookouts, officer of the deck, position plotters, radar operator, bosun, helmsman, and others, two dozen, maybe. When the ship got under way later in the morning, all of them would be doing familiar jobs. Pete would be doing his for the first time. He'd assumed command a month before, but this would be the first time he'd take *his* aircraft carrier to sea. Pete was so hyped and full of energy he thought he might be able to hover.

Aircraft carrier COs weren't supposed to be excitable, though. Instead of sweating, they exuded cool through their pores.

Be cool, Pete.

He crossed the pilothouse to the forward port corner to his chair. Enough light came through the bridge windows to read the white letters sewn into the blue Naugahyde chair cover.

Capt. Pete Adler

Son of a gun! Little Petey Adler, you've come a long way, baby!

To the west it was still black, above blue, and to the east red and orange.

Pete clasped his hands behind him and regarded the San Diego–Coronado Bridge towering over the bay. Its tall center pylons rose out of the black water like arms offering the bridge roadbed up to heaven.

An aircraft carrier CO!

He thought he, too, should offer up something to God for all the blessings that had come his way, and for him to be there, in *his* pilothouse, watching July 5, 1988, dawn over San Diego harbor.

Whenever he thought of offering something to God, sacrificing to Him, invariably an image came to mind of a white-haired, white-bearded Abraham, Bowie knife raised, about to stab Isaac tied to an altar atop a hill in the land of Moriah. The thought of sacrificing one of his daughters, or his one and only squeeze, left him shaking his head. Pete owed Him, no question there. He snapped to attention and saluted with his eyes raised to the sky.

Pete hoped He wasn't too disappointed that his faith wasn't up to Abraham's, that all he brought to offer was a puny salute.

Off to the right of the bridge, the red spires atop parts of the Hotel del Coronado pointed to the realm of his disappointed God.

An image of Pop lit up behind Pete's eyeballs. The disappointed look on image-Pop's face said Pete still didn't amount to anything and that his father's assessment hadn't changed since Pete was in second grade.

Pete hadn't thought about those days for six years, when his momma died.

Why the hell you coming back now, Pop?

5

PETEY

IT MUST HAVE STARTED EARLIER, but Pete's memories were fuzzy prior to second grade. Clarity began at age seven, the age of reason, the age at which his guardian angel started chiseling each and every sin on his eternal and everlasting soul.

Sins came as thoughts, words, or deeds. Sins could be things a person did, or failed to do.

Second grade, right after the 1948 World *Serious*, which is what he'd called it then, ended.

On school days, when the church bell chimed three, seventy-eight kids plus Petey Adler spewed out the door and down the steps in the center of Holy Martyrs Catholic Grade School, a spill of noise as well as mass prison break. The escapees sorted themselves into after-school-walk-home groupings. Petey had two choices: Willie Ochsenzeimer, one of four farm boys in his second-grade class, or Jimmie Joe Kleinhammer, a first-grader who lived on the opposite side of town from him.

When he walked with Willie, they skirted the south fence of the cemetery and took Church Street down the hill, across Highway 40 to the west end of Main Street, where Petey lived, and where Willie crossed the bridge over Cowmire Creek and trekked another mile and a half to his dad's farm on the edge of the Mississippi River floodplain. Willie talked about pigs as if his voice was desert-thirsty for an ear. Petey heard about pig poop, slopping pigs, and how to win the blue hog ribbon at the county fair. Petey was always glad when he could grab Jimmie Joe before Willie snagged him. Jimmie Joe loved baseball. Baseball-talk beat pig-talk, for sure.

One Wednesday, Petey latched onto Jimmie Joe. They passed the front of the church and followed the sidewalk between the eastern fence around the cemetery and the nuns' house. Jimmie Joe mentioned how swell it would be when they got to be third-graders.

Petey agreed. "With third, fourth, and fifth grades to pick teams from, we can have eight or nine guys on a side."

"Yeah," Jimmie Joe said, "teams with two infielders, two outfielders, and a pitcher is stupid. Everybody gets a hit."

"Stupid. It's like—"

Petey saw Sister Everest, the first- and second-grade teacher, standing on the concrete porch fronting the convent. She was there to guard walk-home students from the Fant boys. Petey felt as if an ice cube had suddenly solidified in his stomach.

Hank Fant was in third grade, a short, skinny kid, about Sister Everest's size. He always wore his belt with an extra hole punched in it and enough leather dangling from the buckle to go halfway around him a second time. Kids called him the Weasel. His brother Dick was huge and into his fourth stab at completing first grade. Sometimes the Weasel grabbed a girl's lunch box and hurled it across the fence into the cemetery. Mostly, he liked to fight with boys, even though he was smaller than half the first-graders. If he didn't win quickly he'd say, "Get him," to Dick.

The nuns took turns on Fant guard.

Sister Everest stared straight ahead, her lips pressed to a hard line in her scrunched-up face, peering out of the white window atop the black impregnable tower her habit seemed to be.

"Good afternoon, Sister," Jimmie Joe said. She didn't move. She didn't respond.

"You shouldn't have said anything," Petey whispered. "She can't punish me for being polite."

As much as Jimmie Joe liked to hear himself talk, Petey was glad he didn't know anything about pigs.

From the corner of the cemetery fence, a long flight of concrete steps led down to Maple Street. The steps were there for the girls. Boys used the path worn in the dirt next to the steps. As they descended, Jimmie Joe talked about Warren Spahn. Petey half listened but mostly watched for Fants.

From the foot of Church Hill, Maple Street led past one house on the right, between fallow fields, crossed the highway, passed the picnic grounds, and bisected Main Street of St. Ambrose, Missouri. No sidewalks bordered Maple, so pedestrians walked in the street.

Ahead of them, two gaggles of older girls had almost reached the highway where there were no fences or bushes for the Fants to hide behind. Petey glanced to his right up a three-rut dirt road that led into the trees and screened five trailers, one of which housed the Fant boys and their mother. Petey was ready to run if he saw them.

"I'm going to be a pitcher, like Bob Lemon," Jimmie Joe said.

"Let's run," Petey said.

"What?"

"Let's run to the highway."

Jimmie Joe looked up the dirt road toward the hidden trailers. No one was on the road. He shrugged.

"Warren Spahn and Bob Feller are good, but sometimes they're not lucky. I'm going to be good like Bob Lemon and lucky like him too," Jimmie Joe said.

Emmy Lou Hoover's house—she was one of four second-grade girls—occupied the corner of Maple Street and the trailer park dirt road. In front and in back of her house, large cedar bushes flanked steps up to porches, a screened one in the rear, open in front.

They were next to the Hoovers' front yard. No Fant boys in sight. The feeling that they ought to run was almost strong enough to launch Petey whether Jimmie Joe came along or not. Almost.

"Bob Lemon was in the navy. I'm going to be a sailor when I grow up. Then I'll be a pitcher."

Petey cast a quick look behind them. He heard, "Get 'em."

Panic spurred him, but Dick Fant burst from behind the cedar bush at the corner of the Hoover house. He grabbed Petey's arm and jerked him to a stop. He latched onto Jimmie Joe too.

The Weasel came out from behind the bush. Petey saw his eyes and peed his pants. The Weasel sniffed and checked the front of Jimmie Joe's pants and then Petey's. He smiled.

"Albert Adler is the biggest sissy-man in St. Ambrose," the Weasel said. "You wanna fight, Petey Pee-pants?"

"Fight him," Jimmie Joe said. "He called your dad a sissy." "Pop's not a sissy."

"Sure he is." The Weasel got in Petey's face. "The guys at the cork-ball cage behind the American Legion said so. During the old-guys-against-young-guys football game last Sunday, only under-fifty man in town who didn't play was your dad. Well, Sam Grossman. Grossman's too fat to play football. But at least he goes into Bud's Tavern and the American Legion and drinks beer. Your dad's a pussy-whipped sissy. Your momma won't let him drink beer. That's what they said."

"Hit him," Jimmie Joe said.

Petey didn't want to hit him. He was trying to understand how his pop could be a sissy. Petey was as scared of him as he was of nuns and the Fants.

"Let Kleinhammer go," the Weasel said.

Jimmie Joe clenched his fists and glared at the smaller Fant boy.

The Weasel laughed at him. "You going to fight Dick and me over Petey Pee-pants?"

Jimmie Joe looked at Petey and then shook his head, turned, and walked toward the highway.

The Weasel's hard, dark beady eyes nailed Petey to the street. "We can't let him go home to his momma with pissed-in pants," the Weasel said.

Just beyond the Hoovers' backyard a two-foot ditch bordered Maple. A couple of inches of scummy water covered the muddy bottom. Weasel hooked his thumb at it. "Throw him in," he said to his brother.

Petey couldn't remember climbing out of the ditch. Running home with the rotten-egg smell in his nose, his feet squishing his soggy socks, and the book bag his momma sewed for him banging against his leg: vivid recollections.

He passed Jimmie Joe. "Petey, wait."

He ran faster and didn't even look when he crossed the highway. He raced by the clumps of older kids. The girls' gabble stopped as he flew by. One said, "Phew. He stinks." The rest of them giggled.

At Main and Maple, with the American Legion on one corner and Kleinhammer's new grocery store under construction opposite, he turned left, ran past Marcella Mengele's Hair Salon, the volunteer firehouse, Kleinhammer's current store, Grossman's funeral parlor, and then cut through the empty lot. When he rounded the corner at the rear of the house by the cistern, Petey let loose and bawled as loud as he could. It didn't take long. His momma opened the door.

"Petey, what happened?"

"Fants," he yelled, and he went back to sobbing.

"There, there." She hugged him and didn't seem to mind the stink and the mud. "Pop gets home, I'll tell him."

Pop worked at the Farmers' Co-operative Elevator. He stayed late that night loading grain into freight cars. Petey was asleep before he came home.

"Wake up," and the lights coming on jerked Petey out of a deep dark hole with his heart pounding.

Petey squinted through fingers over his eyes. His pop stood in the doorway, filling it.

"You come home bawling, you vex your momma," he said. "Do not vex your momma." He glared at Petey for a moment, turned out the light, and pulled the door shut.

Petey grabbed himself to keep from wetting the bed.

The next day he walked home from school with Willie and heard about hog butchering. Willie described his dad leaning over the animal with a .22 and aiming right between the eyes and then moving the aim-point up two or three inches and *blam.* Then his uncle hustled up and sliced the hog's throat with a razor-sharp butcher knife, and Willie had to hustle, too, to catch the hog's blood in a pan.

"Is that how you make blood sausage?" Petey asked.

Willie laughed. "The look on your face! Man." He paused, but only a second.

"Best when you can shoot the pig on a slope." Willie seemed to think it was awfully important Petey get these details exactly right. "Pig's ass got to be up-slope, course, else it don't work. But you get that carcass situated on a slant, slit that throat, and it's a gusher."

Petey watched Willie walk right in the center of the one-lane bridge over Cowmire Creek, and then he ran around the house and entered the kitchen. His momma was scrubbing clothes in a tub set on two kitchen chairs.

"I'm going to be a Jew," he said. "They were the original Catholics, so that's okay, isn't it?"

That evening as his momma dished up Pop's supper, she said, "Petey said the cutest thing."

Petey got that ice cube in his belly again. He didn't want Pop to know why he wasn't eating pork any more.

When Momma was done telling the story, his pop got that look on his face, and until that moment, Petey had never realized it was just how Sister Everest looked at first- and second-grade boys.

Petey kept his eyes on the table right in front of him until he finished dessert. Then he got up to scrape plates.

"You can leave the plates, Petey," his momma said. "You're going with Pop to get a haircut."

"Take him to Marcella's Hair Salon," Pop growled.

"Albert!" He'd never heard his momma use a nun's voice before. She smiled at Petey. "Wash up. Then go with Pop."

Feldemann's Barber Shop was across Main from the Adler apartment. On Thursdays, Oscar Feldemann went home for supper, but he reopened by seven and stayed as long as he had customers. Pop and Petey were every-other-Thursday-evening regulars. That night a man—he'd played on the young guys' football team while Mr. Feldemann played for the old guys— sat in the chair. When they entered, Mr. Feldemann nodded to Petey's pop while he continued to vigorously stir up lather with the brush in the mug.

There were two barber chairs in the shop, but Petey'd never seen two barbers there. Mr. Feldemann used the chair farthest from the door. His pop sat down on one of the four wire-back, round-seat chairs. Petey scooted up onto the one next to him and watched Mr. Feldemann wipe shaving cream from around his customer's ear.

The bell over the door jangled, and Hank Fant walked in and closed the door behind him.

"You getting a haircut?" Mr. Feldemann asked.

The Weasel didn't answer. He walked up in front of Petey's pop and kicked him hard in the shin.

"Hey." Mr. Feldemann snapped a finger full of shaving cream onto the floor, and, brandishing the razor aloft, started toward the Weasel.

Petey sat, transfixed, and watched. Hank thrust his face forward, hauled off, and kicked his pop a second time. Again, his Pop didn't move. He just stared straight ahead, as if the Weasel wasn't even there.

Why don't you grab the rotten kid? At least shake him some. The Weasel is right. Pop really is a sissy.

Mr. Feldemann grabbed Hank by the back of his coat, hoisted him off the floor, tossed his razor down on to the counter under the room-length half-wall mirror, pulled the door open, and shoved Hank out the door. He landed on his rear.

"Go to hell!" Hank shouted.

Mr. Feldemann took a step toward him, and the Weasel beat it.

"You come back, I'll take a switch to you," Mr. Feldemann yelled, closed the door, turned, and fixed his blue eyes on Petey.

Petey squirmed on the chair, wondering why the barber was looking at him the way he did.

Pop's the sissy.

6

COMMANDER HAROLD PENNINGTON III

An aircraft carrier is honking big: one thousand feet long and one hundred thousand tons, with a five-thousand-man crew.

Harry stood on the flight deck near the ramp and peered down at the puny ship tied up behind the *Marianas.* Before Pearl Harbor, the USS *Missouri* was the cat's whiskers. Since then, flattops ruled the waves. The Japanese signed the World War II surrender document on the deck of the Mighty Mo—once mighty. In a week, she'd be towed to Hawaii and turned into a museum.

Perhaps, Clean Harry, you should get your mind on the business at hand.

A few years before, Harry had visited a mentor, Captain Marsden, on the bridge of his carrier.

"There are 3,500 compartments in this carrier," the captain said. "I can guarantee you, in one of them there's an anonymous pothead screw-off doing something stupid or criminal that puts this whole ship in jeopardy. If I just knew which compartment to go to, I'd go there and shoot the SOB."

Captain Marsden may have been right, but Harry knew that Pete didn't look at things that way. Pete trusted his crew right up until they committed some offense that warranted Captain's Mast. Then he tended to punish the miscreant with a heavy hand. Pete awarded maximum punishments more often than not.

"Captain's Mast is serious business, XO," Pete told him. "Before you send someone to Mast, I want you to be 99.5 percent sure the guy is guilty. But if the people below you filled out a report on one of their subordinates, you have to take that seriously too. Don't dismiss the charge unless you are 95 percent sure he is innocent. If you think the man is guilty, send him on to me. I will convince myself he is guilty, or innocent, using those same confidence levels. If a man is guilty, I intend to hammer him. I want him to not want to come see me at Mast ever again. In our business, we don't have time to deal with three-time losers before we throw them away. We'll give a man a chance, but he better get the message with his first dose of military justice."

Harry smiled.

The little shit is something.

Harry had learned a lot from Pete in a couple of weeks, but one of the things he'd brought with him to his XO job was the notion that he, Harry Pennington, needed to find those anonymous screw-offs and stop them before they committed punishable offenses.

Harry walked to the starboard side and peered down at the flurry of activity on the pier. Last-minute fresh food, airplane spare parts, ship equipment spares, training squadron personnel...a lot of people and things tried to cram themselves aboard at the last minute.

He watched a bus disgorge a line of sailors, probably from the training squadron at Miramar Naval Air Station. A number of the sailors were female. The XO shook his head.

Politicians were pushing more and more women into the services. To Harry, being in the navy meant carrying war to the enemy's country. In peacetime you trained to fight. The politicians pushing for the inclusion of women seemed to be pushing for more constituents earning a federal paycheck instead of pushing for a fiercer brand of warrior.

Some women sailors would be good warriors, some wouldn't.

Harry acknowledged to himself that plenty of male sailors didn't get the warrior thing either.

That's why leadership is so damned important.

He checked his watch. An hour until getting under way.

Come on, XO, let's go find a doper.

Hell, I didn't talk to myself before they made me an executive officer.

7

COLLEEN

She was back in Pete's parking spot.

"The officer of the deck is shifting his watch from the quarterdeck to the bridge." The announcement blared over the ship's PA system and echoed off the pier-side buildings.

Sailors on the pier removed mooring lines from bollards.

Men on the deck of the carrier pulled them aboard. "Shift colors."

A flag unfurled from the mast atop the island, and she knew the one that had been flying from the sternpost would have been hauled down at the same instant. That's how it was done.

From the other side of the carrier, a tugboat tooted its whistle. Tugs did that to acknowledge a pilot's direction, Pete had told her.

Her heart slipped in a couple of extra beats, and she raised her hand to her chest to calm the giddy organ. Her eyes were wet. She was happy and proud and with him, but not. He was up there behind the glare-shuttered windows of the pilothouse, and although she knew some sailor things, she didn't have a clue as to all the minute and detailed chores and tasks the dozens of people on the bridge would be doing.

She reached up to touch the windshield.

Pete had told her, when he fell asleep he liked to have his hand on her hip. Otherwise he often had a dream that he was falling off the world and would jerk awake. On cruise, he put his hand on an angle iron next to his bunk. "And that connects me through the ship, through the sea, to the shore, and through the earth to where you are. It works. I haven't fallen off the planet yet."

A rap on the window startled her.

Captain Abner Barton grinned in the window at her. She opened the door, and he held his hand out to help her down.

Abner was the chief of staff for Vice Admiral Warren. The vice admiral commanded all naval aircraft and aircraft carriers on the west coast.

"The admiral letting you play hooky, Abner?" Colleen asked him.

"Doesn't happen very often, but once in a while, he lets me slip out for a few moments."

Abner shielded his eyes and looked up at the bridge windows of the *Marianas* as she inched away from the pier.

"You know, Colleen, I met Pete ten years ago at the start of a cruise out to the Indian Ocean. I thought he was a feisty little son-of-a-gun. By the end of the cruise, I knew he was going to go places in the navy. I was glad to see him get a carrier."

Colleen looked up at Abner. He was taller than Pete, but more slender. Reddish-brown hair on top, gray on the side. Gray mustache.

She never knew how to respond when someone complimented Pete.

"You know what happened when Pete got the call that he screened?"

"Sure. I was on the phone with the admiral when he told Pete. After we hung up, the admiral was surprised that Pete didn't react. 'What was that?' he asked me. 'Did someone tell him? Maybe he thought he deserved it. Don't tell me we just screened a flaming arrogant prick for carrier command.'"

"Let me tell you the rest of the story, as Paul Harvey would say."

She did, including Eileen's fribble-frappin' math. Abner laughed.

"You mind if I tell this story to the admiral?" "Pete would say, it's what happened."

The carrier was angled forty-five degrees, bow away from the pier, and turning more rapidly through its one-eighty to line up with the outbound track.

"Best be getting back. Great to see you, Colleen." "You too, Abner."

Colleen climbed back in and started the car. "For those in peril on the sea."

She decide not to tack on the amen.

8

CAPTAIN PETE ADLER

As tugs inched the *Marianas* away from the pier, separating her from the shore, Pete recalled something his XO had told him.

"My sea daddy's words of wisdom," Harry said.

Harry's mentor had told him that at any given moment, in one of any carrier's many compartments, some screw-off was smoking dope and endangering the ship and crew.

Pete was new to the carrier but not new to command. Previously, he commanded an amphibious ship, an airwing, and an A-7 aircraft squadron. He had plenty of experience with sailors and the kinds of trouble they could cause. Harry's friend may have been right. At that very moment, while the crew was engaged in the delicate process of getting under way, there could be a pothead screw-off somewhere below endangering the ship, but Pete considered himself to be more a "glass half-full" guy. He believed he could pick fifty sailors off his ship, stick them in a trench, toss a grenade in, and be able to count on forty-nine of them to do the right thing. He hoped he wasn't overconfident in his forty-nine and underworried about the XO's sea daddy's one. Maneuvering a floating airport out of the confined harbor took the efforts of a lot of officers and sailors doing specific tasks. Pete was the only one in the pilothouse without a specific job to do, but if the OOD, the helmsman, or any one of the sailors on the navigation team screwed up and the ship ran aground or collided with another vessel, it would be Pete's fault.

It worked that way in the navy.

The ship was about forty feet from the pier. It was a gloriously clear, blue-sky day, but the navigation team acted as if it was socked in pea-soup fog. The air carried an electrostatic charge. The hair on Pete's arms tingled. He could hear the tension. The navigation team spoke a precise, professional shorthand in muted, earnest, almost reverent voices.

"Starboard engine ahead two-thirds. Port engine back two-thirds." The officer of the deck's drill-instructor voice stomped roughshod over the buzz. The sailor stationed next to the helmsman parroted the order; then he passed the OOD's direction to the engine rooms.

Pete's cheek muscles twitched, containing the smile that was trying to sneak onto his cool-carrier-CO face. Pete thought the navigation team was pretty close to satisfactory. When navy pilots land aboard aircraft carriers, each landing is graded. The highest grade awarded is an OK. To Pete, satisfactory was the same as high praise.

Tugboats had the *Marianas* far enough away from the pier to begin turning the ship through 180 degrees to line up with the outbound channel. Pete hopped down from his chair and hurried through the press of bodies to the starboard side. Colleen had planned to return to see them off.

Their blue Chevy van sat in the CO's spot. He couldn't see her on the pier. Sun glinted off the windshield, so he couldn't tell if she was inside, either.

He became aware that his heart was beating fast. Probably afire with the notion of going out to sea and doing stuff mortal, earthbound, shore-duty pukes couldn't even dream of doing. Leaving Colleen tugged at him also. He wanted one more glimpse of her. He amended one of his earlier musings: *We've come a long way, baby.* It was right to include her. Since the navy and he had married her, the two of them had brought her plenty of *for worses* to weather. Carrier CO's wife, finally, a *for better.*

See you in a couple of days, Colleen.

Pete pulled his eyes away from the pier and watched the bow swinging. The island on the USS *Marianas* was situated two-thirds of the length of the carrier back from the end of the flight deck and on the starboard side. For driving the ship, it would have been better to have the island in the center of the deck, but that would have screwed up the arrangement of the takeoff and landing area.

The edge of the flight deck hid several hundred feet directly in front of the ship from view on the bridge. A small boat would disappear under the edge of the flight deck a long ways before the ship reached it. The problem was, from the bridge, a person couldn't see if the boat got out of the way or not. There were a few things a man had to get used to on a carrier bridge.

As soon as they steadied on the first outbound leg, Pete paid close attention to where the ship was really pointed. With the island on the starboard side of the huge ship, the perspective was funky. Pete's mind wanted to believe the ship was moving in the direction the bow pointed, but the track the ship followed was actually to the right of the bow. Funky, but it made sense, given the location of the island.

The tugboats cast off, and the OOD ordered ten knots. Pete stood on the starboard side and watched the crew go through their paces.

"I hold us ten yards left of track, based on good fixes," the navigator said. "Recommend coming left to two-four-zero." Gator's voice was just as loud as the OOD's, but it lacked the power and authority. Pete had been on the bridge of a US Navy ship many times while entering and leaving port, but he'd never noticed that subtle tone of voice difference before. "Recommend," Gator said. The OOD commanded.

After making the next turn, the ship had a straight shot out to sea. Pete slid between bodies, crossed to the port side, and climbed up onto his chair. The pilothouse was wide enough such that the perspective of the bow and the heading of the ship were a bit different from the port side. He regarded the bow, noted how the ship moved down the channel, and it clicked.

Pete had been confident that he could handle the carrier CO job. He believed all twenty-eight of his years in the navy, six of them enlisted, and all his previous assignments had been to prepare him for the carrier CO job. Still, until a man actually does it, there's doubt.

"Morning, Cap'n." The exec approached. "Clean Harry."

Most navy vessels used dark green tile in passageways and mess decks. After Pete told him he wanted a clean ship, Clean Harry had white tile installed and demanded that the white tile glisten.

"Day like this, you know where the saying comes from, 'Sailors are meant to be on ships…'"

"'…and ships are meant to be at sea.'" Pete finished the XO's saying.

"Chief engineer wanted me to ask if you've decided whether he could conduct engineering casualty drills this afternoon. Just minor stuff, Cheng says. No chance of a problem that would cause us to have to stop flight operations."

Aircraft carriers are engineering marvels, but they are complex and packed with volatile fuel and explosives. Things fail, fuel pipes leak, sailors and officers make mistakes. Crews have to be able to respond to engineering plant problems rapidly and with the precise antidote for the specific casualty. Good chief engineers practiced their crews relentlessly. There were times, though, when practice to handle an imagined failure induced a real one. Sometimes a sailor pushed the wrong button when attempting to correct a minor problem, and the small issue blew up into a total power failure. Things were dicey enough during flight operations without risking a drill-induced equipment casualty in the mix.

"Yep. I decided. No engineering drills. This isn't a Monday, but it is right after a holiday. They can drill tonight after flight ops."

The XO's face lit up. "Great minds," he said. "How's refurbing the admiral's quarters coming?"

The XO snorted. "His aide called me ten minutes before we

pulled the phone lines. Admiral Miller wants a padded seat on the toilet in his head before he comes to sea with us in two weeks."

"You're kidding."

"No, Cap'n. Not kidding. But Clean Harry's all over it. Permission to strike below, sir?"

The XO left and Pete thought of another of the ubiquitous sailor sayings: *It's better to be lucky than good.*

He was sure lucky to have Clean Harry as exec and Fireball Freddie Fosdick as chief engineer. He looked forward to evaluating the ops officer and the Air Boss, two other key department heads, during the at sea period. They had good reps, but seeing them in action was the only thing that counted.

To starboard, the brown dirt of Point Loma rose above the top of the window. Straight ahead, a sailboat, a kelp-trawler, and a forty-footer owned by a legitimately rich person or a drug dealer, maybe, preceded the carrier out of the channel.

Pete thought he was a long way south of rich, but from his seat in the pilothouse, he could look out his windows on something with a lot more value than any rich person owned, even if it was his for only eighteen months. An aircraft carrier— nothing on the face of God's blue earth was worth more. Nobody whose opinion mattered would argue against that notion.

Pop.

His opinion shouldn't matter anymore, for a lot of reasons. It did, though.

The last two channel marker buoys lay just ahead. The kelp trawler had turned right, the sailboat left, and the rich-guy cruiser was still ahead. It began to rise and fall with swells and waves and spew white spray away from the bow.

The OOD marched over and saluted. "Cap'n, permission to secure the special navigation detail and set the regular underway watch."

"Make it so." Pete returned the salute.

The bosun keyed the mic to the ship's announcing system. "Set the regular underway watch. On deck section one."

Pete exhaled. *Piece of cake getting an aircraft carrier under way.*

"Coffee, Cap'n?"

Impeccably attired, meticulously groomed, blond buzz cut, lean six-footer Lance Corporal Solomon, the CO's orderly, extended a coffee mug. At first glance, Solomon wore the face of a boy. A second look discovered cold, hard blue eyes.

Besides sailors, an aircraft carrier carried a contingent of marines. One of them was assigned to be the commanding officer's orderly. Generally a junior man, but not a raw recruit, filled the billet. Lance corporal, the third enlisted rank.

Pete took a sip. "Ambrosia. Thanks, Lance Corporal."

"Sir," he said, resuming his position at the rear of the pilothouse at parade rest.

"Coming up to twenty-two knots, Captain," the OOD said from the center of the pilothouse. They'd briefed twenty-two knots for the transit to the operating area, and the OOD really didn't need to inform him. But the officers and crew didn't know the new CO yet. The OOD was playing it carefully.

As the ship accelerated, Pete felt those thousands of horsepower cranking the propellers faster and faster. *Man! Aircraft carriers are something, even when we're not flying airplanes.*

"Fire, fire. Fire in the number one engine room." The announcement blared over the ship's PA system.

Holy Mary, Mother of God, pray for us sinners…

9

COMMANDER HAROLD PENNINGTON III

A FIRE! GODDAMN!

Harry was in his stateroom, the bathroom, actually.

The very worst thing that could happen to an XO was to be caught with his pants down. Harry muttered an impressive string of expletives and got his pants back up. He washed his hands; then he grabbed his handheld radio.

"Damage Control Central, you up?" "We're not manned yet, XO."

Sanchez, a good kid. "What do you know, Sanchez?"

"Just that there's been a fuel leak in number one engine room and that it torched."

"As soon as Commander Fosdick gets there, tell him to call me."

"Aye, sir."

Harry's stateroom was on the port side aft. The entrance to number one engine room was on the starboard side and forward. He hurried out, joined the hordes thundering aft down the passageway to the first cross-ship walkway, turned left, crossed to starboard, and joined the forward hustling crew on the other side.

In a large fire, the crew was called to battle stations, and then the ship would be buttoned up to contain battle damage, fire, flooding, and fumes.

The bridge hadn't called the ship to battle stations. Maybe the fire could be contained with the damage-control crews.

Harry reached the entrance to number one engine room. Chief Petty Officer Cooper, a damage control specialist, stood with his back to the bulkhead.

"Status," Harry barked to the chief.

"The crew from number one said they found fuel floating in the bilges. Before they could respond, it torched off. They evacuated the space and tripped the Halon System. Far as I can tell, the Halon snuffed the fire. All I know, XO."

Harry nodded. "Where are they, the guys from number one?"

"I sent 'em to the hangar bay, sir."

Harry hurried forward and found a ladder leading up a level.

10

CAPTAIN PETE ADLER

A FIRE!

Through the steel, a hundred feet below, Pete imagined them: hordes of sailors running to their stations. Fire was their enemy. Fire had a nose for fuel and ammo. The ship's tanks held millions of gallons. Magazines stored thousands of tons. Time was the enemy. The crew knew: no shoving, no talking. Purposeful, practiced hauling ass to their stations. Some stomped up ladders with a sound like rolling thunder. Others rumbled down.

They had jobs.

I'm sitting on my dad-burned chair. And it's not a *fire, it's* my *fire!*

Mechanical failure, an honest mistake, a bonehead action by a brain-fried doper—the cause didn't matter. Sailors killed or injured, equipment damaged and destroyed, dollars lost: Pete was responsible, and he was sitting on his stupid chair.

He climbed down. *There, a productive act.*

The crew was good. They trained for every conceivable emergency.

Pete looked around the pilothouse. The navigation team hovered over their charts. The helmsman concentrated on his compass. Phone talkers buzzed into their mouthpieces. The OOD looked through binocs at a sailboat off the starboard bow.

What the hell is going on below? Why don't I get a report?

Number one engine room. Pete pictured it. The fuel pipes ran through the bilges. A burst fuel pipe, maybe. Lots of things hot enough to torch off a spill. The crew could smother a bilge fire with foam. The crew would know what to do. Even without number one, they had three other engine rooms. The ship ran fine on three.

What the hell is hap—

"Damage Control Central manned." The phone talker stood just behind the helmsman.

In an emergency, the chief engineer took charge of DC Central. Fireball Freddie Fosdick would get a handle on the fire location and severity, develop a plan to fight it, organize firefighting teams, and direct their efforts.

Fireball Fred was one of the best.

Crap! The ship was going twenty-two knots.

Get your stuff together, CO. "CO" felt like it had come from his pop.

"OD," Pete said, "ten knots." Sometimes even three-letter acronyms were too cumbersome.

The navigator was on the starboard side by the plotting table.

"Gator, soon as we've got deep water, turn south. Keep us close to North Island," Pete said.

On his previous ship, when he encountered problems in the engineering plant, Pete'd learned to check the smoke coming out of the stack. Black smoke was dangerous; white smoke, very dangerous.

"OOD, I'm going aft to check the smokestack. Don't run into anybody, and don't run aground."

Lieutenant Harlan Zerjav, the OOD, was a good ship driver. Pete'd hurt his feelings. His face showed it. He knew what to do.

No time for hurt feelings.

The CO started crossing the pilothouse.

"OOD," a phone talker called out, "Damage Control Central reports number one engine room has been abandoned and the Halon system has been activated."

Crap! Not a little one.

Halon was a last resort. It displaced the oxygen and smothered a fire in a confined space. But what caused it? If Fireball knew, he'd report it. If the XO knew, he'd call. He decided not to bug them.

Pete started leaving, stopped again, and directed the navigator to assign one of his sailors the task of keeping a log of everything related to the fire. Every ship kept a log of navigation, weather, and other pertinent operational details. If the Halon system was activated, they were dealing with a big fire. Pete thought a log of fire-specific events could be important. Fireball would have a log going in DC Central, but he was deep inside the ship. In the pilothouse, they had windows and saw things they couldn't from below.

As he left to check the smokestack, thoughts flitted through his head.

They'll probably use my fire log against me during my court martial.

One thing matters, Pete Adler. Don't kill anybody with your *fire.*

A catwalk skirted the starboard side of the island aft of the pilothouse. He looked up at the smokestack, and his heart skipped a thump or two. A massive stream of white smoke spewed out of the stack fifty feet above him.

Could be steam. They'd shut down the boilers in the number one. The boilers had safety valves that vented off excess steam.

Back inside, he called the chief engineer, told him what he'd seen.

"We have a video camera aimed at the stack. I know it's white. It's steam."

Fireball was in hurry. He wanted to get back to figuring out what the hell went wrong. Also, he probably thought Pete was just a new-guy CO. Stupid aviator to boot. What could he know about fighting fires on ships?

The control tower was aft in the island and on the same level as the pilothouse. The air boss ran the tower. Pete called him on the phone.

"Boss, your aviation fuel guys weren't pumping fuel, were they?"

"No, sir. We weren't due to start pumping for another five minutes."

"Okay." Pete almost hung up. "Check. Make sure somebody didn't jump the gun. Check; then call me."

Fireball called on the phone. "I just got a report from the chief petty officer in charge of the number one engine room. One of his watch standers reported fuel floating in the bilges. Shortly after that, they saw burning fuel cascading down the sides of the boilers. The chief ordered the crew to shut down and evacuate the space. The chief tripped the Halon and secured the hatch."

"How the hell can fuel get up there, to run down from on top?"

"Don't know yet, Cap'n. Aviation fuel lines run through the space above number one, but the flyboys hadn't started pumping yet. So it's got to be engineering fuel. Our fuel lines run through the bilges. But in twenty-five years, there've been upgrades. Sometimes they saved money and didn't update the diagrams. I don't know what the problem is yet. We're working like hell to get it figured."

Pete called the Boss and got, "Not us."

Petty Officer Medina had been assigned to keep the fire log.

Pete asked to see it.

Fire Log, 5 July 1988 (PO3 Juan Medina)

> 1100: Fire in number one engine room announced. 1101: Slowed from twenty-two to ten knots.
>
> 1103: DC Central manned and ready.
>
> 1102: Number one engine room shut down and abandoned. Halon system activated. (reported at 1104)

Pete told Medina to add the details he'd gotten from the chief engineer, his conversations with the air boss, and that the CO observed billowing white smoke or steam from the smokestack.

Watch check: 1107! It felt like it should be 1500. The XO called on the walkie-talkie.

"Anybody hurt?" Pete asked. "No, sir. Everyone got out okay." "Where are you?"

"Second deck, right by the escape hatch from number one. I was on the hangar bay. Talked to the guys from number one. I called Fred and he said he called you. I just got down here."

"Deck hot? Any indication the fire's still going?"

"No. Appears the Halon did the job...Cap'n, you might want to call Rear Admiral Miller. Vice Admiral Warren's chief of staff too. On the cellular telephone. Just to let them know what's going on. Also, I told Ops O to push back flight operations two hours and to work up a situation report together with the chief engineer."

I should have thought of that.

Encounter a problem at sea and the people on a ship fixate on solving the problem. Inform an admiral of a problem right away, usually he responds, "What can I do to help?" If he's blindsided, then it's, "What the hell have those idiots done now?" There was a cellular telephone on a shelf in front of the CO's chair. Cellular telephones. Pete'd never seen one until he checked aboard the carrier. It was the size of a small briefcase, most of it battery. Phil Proctor, his predecessor, had bought three.

He called his boss's office. A third-class petty officer answered. Pete asked for Admiral Miller, then his chief of staff, then any staff officer.

"I'm the only one here," the petty officer responded.

Where the hell are they? Pete wondered, along with a few other questions he didn't have time for.

"We have a fire on the *Marianas.* Make sure the admiral gets the message."

Pete left the number of his cellular phone, hung up, and dialed Captain Abner Barton, Vice Admiral Warren's chief of staff, and a friend. Pete told him about the fire, what they knew, and what they were still trying to figure out.

"Need something, ask," Abner said.

If you were here, Phil, I'd kiss you on the lips—um, belay that last part.

Pete informed the XO and chief engineer of the phone call, made sure Medina had the fire log up to date, and checked with the OOD and the navigator.

The ship was eight miles off the coast, well clear of the channel into the harbor. One other ship, a navy destroyer, two miles closer to shore than *Marianas*, doing practice precision anchoring drills. Navy ships used that spot for the purpose regularly.

Now 1122.

Nobody to call, nothing to do. White smoke worry padded behind him like a satanic hound of heaven. Pete went back to the catwalk.

The white stuff continued to billow. Some of it had to be steam. They had ordered twenty-two knots. The fuel pumps howled at that speed. Made a hot fire. Generated a lot of steam. Then the fire, and the engineers shut down the boilers. A lot of steam with nowhere to go but up the stacks. But they'd been venting it for *thirty minutes.*

How long would it take to vent off a boiler? Shouldn't the flow be diminished, at least? Plenty of goddamned questions. No friggin' answers!

Just then a gust of wind stuffed a whiff of jet fuel up Pete's nose. He looked back up at that billowing white cloud.

Holy Mary, mother of God…

11

CAPTAIN PETE ADLER

BACK IN THE PILOTHOUSE, PETE called Fred and told him he smelled strong fuel vapors coming from the smokestack.

Fred couldn't understand how it could be fuel. It didn't make sense.

"Fuel cascading down from on top of the boiler doesn't make sense either, but you told me that's what the guys reported. Listen to me, Fred. It's fuel vapor along with steam, and we are in big trouble. We have to get this figured out."

Pete hung up and told Medina to bring his log over.

Fire Log (PO3 Medina)

> 1100: Fire in number one engine room announced. 1101: Slowed from twenty-two to ten knots.
>
> 1102: Fuel leak in number one engine room. Burning fuel running down sides of boilers. Shut down boilers. Space abandoned. Halon system activated.
>
> 1103: DC Central manned and ready.
>
> 1105: CO called DC Central to report white smoke from stack. Chief Engineer said white smoke was steam.

1106: Air Boss ensured no jet fuel being pumped. 1107: XO reported no injuries to number one engine room crew. Deck above number one not hot.

Halon appears to have extinguished fire. Flight operations pushed back two hours.

1111: CO called Rear Admiral Miller and Vice Admiral Warren's chief of staff on cellular phone with Sitrep.

1115: This item copied from DC Central log. Chief Engineer called Commander Smedley on Admiral Warren's staff via radio phone-patch. Ship's diagrams show aviation fuel lines running through uptakes above number one engine room. Smedley said those aviation fuel lines were removed twelve years ago. Ship's diagrams not updated.

1120: Ship steaming back and forth ten to twenty miles from North Island Naval Air Station.

1121: Captain left pilothouse to check smokestack. 1124: Captain reported smelling jet fuel from catwalk below smokestack. Informed DC Central and XO. Ordered Air Boss to have aviation fuel pump rooms inspected. Ordered aviation fuels officer to the pilothouse.

"Cap'n." It was the Air Boss and his fuels officer, Warrant Officer Lister. Pete handed the log back to Medina. He smiled and nodded to him.

Watch check: 1134.

As they hustled back to the catwalk, Pete asked the Air Boss, "Who did you send to check the aviation fuel pump rooms?"

"Chief Pratt. I told him to personally visit each pump room and make abso-damn-lutely sure not one of our pumps is turned on."

"May be overkill," Pete said. "According to Cheng, originally, jet fuel piping ran through the uptakes above the boilers. Those lines were rerouted."

"Uh, Cap'n." Warrant Officer Lister started to speak, but Pete opened the door out onto the catwalk, and the Boss and Lister trundled out after him. Pete sniffed, didn't smell anything. All three looked up. Rivulets of liquid trickled down the side of the stack. That was new. Condensed water from the steam? Or…

Pete put his foot on a rung of the ladder leading up the side of the stack.

"Let the warrant go, Cap'n," the Boss said.

Lister was five ten, a rake handle, darkly tanned, squint wrinkled around his eyes, black haired, and a smoker. After climbing ten ladders to the pilothouse, he was huffing. Pete wondered if he could do another but got out of his way.

Lister looked up at those trickles and went up. Halfway to the top, he stopped, swiped a finger through a rivulet, sniffed, and looked down. His face was pale.

"Shit," Lister said, and he rattled down the ladder. The Boss said, "Jet fuel?"

Grim-faced Lister nodded. "The jet fuel additives give it a distinct smell."

"How the hell is jet fuel getting in that smokestack?" Pete asked.

A sailor barged out of the tower, onto the catwalk, and blurted, "Boss, Boss. Chief Pratt called and said to tell you right away. We *were* pumping jet fuel from the after pump room. The Chief made them stop."

Pete's knees buckled. He grabbed a handrail.

Shit. The son of a bitch is solid. I'm not dreaming.

The Boss's guys had pumped jet fuel. Still didn't know how it got in the smoke from the stack. But Pete knew there was a lot of jet fuel in a very wrong place—or places.

"It's 1142. We've been pumping jet fuel for forty-two friggin' minutes? But the chief engineer said the piping doesn't go through the uptakes above the boilers. So how—"

"That fuel pipe repair on the third deck, Cap'n," Lister said. "The one I showed you last week."

"That's the problem? And I looked right at it?"

"It *might* be the problem, Cap'n," Lister said. "Okay if I go check?"

"Go."

Lister left. The sailor went back into the tower. The Boss looked at Pete. There was a lot of stuff on his face. Most of it was *I'd rather be dead than let you down like I just did.* His guys pumped the fuel. And lied to him, which made him tell his CO a lie. "Not us," he'd said.

But Pete had looked at that pipe and said, "Looks okay to me."

If anybody has an unforgiveable sin on his soul, it's me. I'm the goddamned captain. I looked right at that pipe. "Looks okay to me," I said.

Pete knew his previous ship from stem to stern and from mast top to bilge. He could still picture the layout of all the main features. He knew he should have had the *Marianas* in his head like that too. It was so damned big. He could have pushed it harder. Should have. Could have. Preambles to an unforgiveable sin.

When Pete got back to the pilothouse, it occurred to him that he should have said something to the Air Boss.

No goddamned time for hurt feelings.

Pete climbed onto his chair.

The jet fuel guys had busted a rule and pumped fuel early. They were at least part of the problem. Those two things were clear, but they still didn't know what the whole problem was. Even if they pumped early, there shouldn't have been a way for the jet fuel to cause the fire. They didn't know what to fix. Unless it was that pipe repair job he'd looked at the week before.

He waited for Lister to report. On his chair.

I set my carrier on fire. An unforgiveable sin.

Pete leaned back and remembered his first unforgiveable sin.

12

PETEY

Sister Daniels taught third through fifth grades. Before his grade-three September was over, Petey's knuckles met her ruler. The two of them met frequently. When school convened for his fifth grade, Sister Daniels was gone. To the middle-grade boys, her replacement appeared like the miracle of Fatima. Sister Robert smiled. Her pretty young face, gazing radiantly out of the black-and-white wrapping, burned off dreary overcasts and gloomy fogs. She played softball with the girls and, most amazingly, baseball with the boys.

Before school and fifth grade started, Petey began to dread moving into sixth. Jimmie Joe Kleinhammer had developed into a good pitcher. Petey was his catcher. Next year he'd move to a new classroom, and the Kleinhammer-Adler battery would be busted up. That was the bad news, but severely limited in its power by not having happened yet, and of course by the wonder of Sister Robert.

Sister knew baseball inside and out. When she talked about the game, he and Jimmie Joe paid attention.

The boys had no idea nuns could do such things, play baseball and smile. The girls liked her too. By November that year, fourth- and fifth-grade girls began to talk about becoming nuns—maybe.

Petey went to bed Sunday night after Thanksgiving, anticipating recess the next day. On Monday they'd switch from baseball to playing football at noon. The boys figured they'd seen the last of Sister Robert on the playground until the spring. Petey was dreaming of tackling Sam Grossman and making him fumble when his pop pulled him out of bed.

"Leave your jamas on. Grab your school clothes, books, toothbrush," Pop said.

Petey moved around in a daze, gathering stuff. His pop grabbed his arm.

"Toothbrush," he said. "Leave it."

He dragged Petey out to the family's black, two-door Plymouth. The motor was running. He yanked the driver's seat forward, shoved Petey into the rear, slammed the seat back, and got in. Momma was sitting in the passenger seat in front. She was quiet. She didn't move.

"Momma?"

Pop put the car in reverse and backed up. "Don't. Vex." He stopped the car, shifted, and they moved forward. "Your momma."

Petey kept his mouth shut as Pop drove to Uncle Pete's. His uncle waited on the sidewalk between his detached garage and the back porch. He wore bib overalls over long johns.

Pop stopped, jerked Petey out of the car, thrust him and his stuff at Uncle Pete, and then he backed out of the drive.

"What's wrong with Momma?" Petey asked.

Uncle Pete rubbed his big calloused hand through the boy's hair. "Your momma's sick. Your dad's taking her to the hospital. They'll make her better."

He took the book bag and the clothes. "Come on, Petey. Let's get you back to bed."

Petey liked his uncle. His momma had three other brothers and two sisters. The Adlers never visited, never saw them, only Uncle Pete and Aunt Dorothy twice a month for Sunday supper.

Uncle Pete had built a two-story on the first bit of level ground along Church Street below Church Hill. His garden extended from behind his house to a steep wooded slope. Atop the slope, when the leaves were off the trees, a person could see the fence around the cemetery. Petey had an easy walk to school that morning. At Mass he prayed for Momma as Uncle Pete had told him to.

At recess, the boys were in a circle in the center of the football field choosing sides when Sister Robert walked into the middle of the gaggle.

"I'm playing," Sister said.

The "double-dare-ya" smile on her face definitely belonged on the boys' playground, not the girls', where they played dodge ball.

"We play tackle, Sister," Petey pointed out.

She pulled two strips of white rag out of a pocket and tucked them into the sides of the black sash around her waist. "When I carry the ball, grab one of the rags. That counts as a tackle."

Sister Robert wound up on Sam Grossman's team.

Jimmie Joe Kleinhammer held the ball for Petey, and he kicked off. Jimmie Joe covered the right half of the field as a safety tackle. Petey covered the left.

Sister snatched the ball off the ground, herded three blockers in front of her, and positioned herself behind the wedge. Bodies collided, and her blockers and Petey's tacklers all wound up sitting on the ground looking dazed, as though they were asking themselves if football was supposed to hurt.

Sister grabbed a handful of habit and hiked it up. Her black shoes flew. Her black-stockinged knees pumped her down the field in long strides. Willie Ochsenzeimer hunched over, his arms extended in front of him in a half circle, right in Sister's path, perfectly positioned to grab one of the flags, but Sister straight-armed him onto his backside. While she was disposing of Willie on one side, Jimmie Joe grabbed the flag from the other. She'd made it halfway to the goal line.

Sam Grossman tossed a pass to Sister. Next play, she ran the ball and then caught another pass to score.

Sam's team kicked off. Willie fielded the ball, got tackled quickly, and fumbled. Jimmie Joe pounced on the ball. They planned plays away from Sister's side of the field. Petey caught a long pass from Jimmie Joe. Then Jimmie Joe scored on a quarterback keeper.

As they walked back to kickoff again, Petey saw Sister Superior standing on the sidewalk just beyond the end of the field of play. Statue still, hands up the sleeves, the "face'll crack if I smile" look.

What is she doing here?

She never came out to the playground during recess.

But Petey had other things to worry about. He got the team in a huddle and told them to watch out for Sister's tricks.

"Willie," he said, "for a guy who knows as much about pigs as you, you sure don't know about pigskins. Now don't let her straight-arm you again." He thumped a finger against his chest.

Petey kicked off. Sister got the ball, and, like the first time, she sailed through the line of would-be tacklers and drew a bead on Willie. He hunched over, as he had before, but just before Sister's hand wound up in his face, Willie slapped it aside. As she tried to run past him full out, he tackled her.

Willie and Sister hit the ground and rolled, both swallowed by the black cloud of her habit. A giant upside-down bowl of hush covered the playground. From outside the stillness, Petey heard birds chirping and the girls laugh and shout from their playground. He smelled burning leaves.

Willie's head was tangled under Sister's habit. He struggled to get out of there. Sister began laughing. From all over the field, boys started running toward the two of them.

"Stop jerking, Willie," Sister said. "You'll pull my dress off." Willie went still. Running boys stopped. Petey slid to a halt, feeling as if he should drop to his knees and reel off bushels of Our Fathers and Hail Marys. Maybe He should have added *Thou shalt not tackle a nun.*

Sister pulled on the folds of her habit and got Willie free. "Are you okay, Willie?" she asked.

"I don't want to go to hell," Willie howled. "I'm sorry."

He started crying as if the devil already had one of his feet close enough to feel the heat.

"Willie, you're not going to hell. You didn't do anything wrong. I did, and I need to go to confession for it."

Sister hugged Willie for a moment, and when she let him go, a glistening wet spot of tears and snot marked the center of her black chest right below the wimple.

"You didn't do anything wrong, Willie," Sister repeated. "Now finish your game. I need to change." She started brushing dust off her habit and then gave up and headed for the convent.

Sister Superior!

Petey looked up. The spot she had occupied on the sidewalk was empty. He breathed a sigh of relief, and they set about beating the crap out of Sam Grossman's team in the twenty minutes they had left.

Petey was in his place, pleased they'd beaten Grossman's team thirty-six to twelve, when the bell rang. Normally, Sister Robert was there well before the bell, but she wasn't that day. The bell stifled the postrecess clamor. Still Sister didn't enter the room. Voices buzzed and then exploded into cacophony. Sister Superior opened the door and sound ceased. She strode to the chalkboard and wrote columns of assignments in each subject for each grade. When she stabbed a period after the last entry, there was enough homework to carry them through high school.

Sister Superior turned.

"I will read each assignment. If I can't read your penmanship, you will do the assignment over until I can. If it looks like one of you copied another's work, you will all do it over until I am satisfied you are turning in your own work."

Emmy Lou Hoover sat in front of Petey. She raised a hand and asked, "Is Sister Robert okay?"

"I didn't give you permission to speak. Get busy with your assignments."

Sister Superior stepped down from the one-foot-high platform in front of the chalkboard.

"You will not have someone in the room watching you," Sister said. "I am right across the hall. I *will* check on you. You won't know when."

Looking at her cold brown eyes reminded Petey of that "outer darkness" place, where the weeping and gnashing happened. She swept the rows of students with those eyes that seemed eager to find just one tiny fault. Then she closed the door.

Desk lids squeaked. Papers rustled. Petey remembered to breathe.

* * *

After school Petey returned to his uncle's house. Pop visited Momma in the hospital. Then he picked up his son.

His pop walked in the door, and Petey jumped up from the kitchen table where he'd been doing homework.

"Is Momma okay?" "Get in the car."

"Albert. He's a little boy." Aunt Dorothy put her hand on Petey's arm. "Your momma's getting better. Don't worry. She'll be able to come home in a couple of days."

As they drove, his pop didn't say anything. Petey wanted to ask about Momma but was afraid to. At their house, Petey went to his room.

A few minutes elapsed. "Petey."

The way he said the name made Petey's knees tremble. He had never been so afraid, not even of Dick Fant.

A doubled-over razor strop dangled from his hand. His momma had spanked him a time or two, but Pop had never spanked him or whipped him with a belt before. He had never touched Petey. Now, he pointed to a chair positioned in the middle of the floor.

"Lay across that."

The boy looked at him, at the chair, then at the strop.

Pop grabbed the back of his shirt and bent him over the chair. "Don't move." Petey didn't.

He heard the *whap* sound a split second before he felt the sharp slice of pain across his buttocks and flash like lightning behind his eyes. He screamed.

"Shut. Up."

Whap. He gripped the rung of the chair and clenched his teeth and buttocks. *Whap.* He sucked snot into his throat, choked, and coughed. *Whap.* A whimper escaped before he bit it off. "Five. Six," he said, and Petey tensed again.

"Get up."

He turned his head sideways and peered up warily. "Get up, I said."

He stood, and his hands rubbed his butt. His pop held out his red handkerchief. Petey wiped his nose on the sleeve of his shirt.

"Tackling a nun," he said, shaking his head. "That's one a those sins can't ever be forgiven."

"Wasn't me. Willie Ochsenzeimer tackled her."

Pop grabbed the back of his shirt and put him back across the chair. He gave him two more whaps. "You were team captain. So you tackled her too." Two more whaps. "And that's for how you looked at me. Don't you ever, ever look at me like that again." *Whap.*

Petey thought it was getting real hard to hang onto the notion that his pop was a sissy.

13

COMMANDER HAROLD PENNINGTON III

The XO and Commander Fosdick had discussed the cause of the fire and how to explain it.

"Picture's worth, etcetera," Fireball said. Then he sketched the piping layout, which had been one factor that caused the fire.

Harry took it up to the pilothouse to show it to the CO.

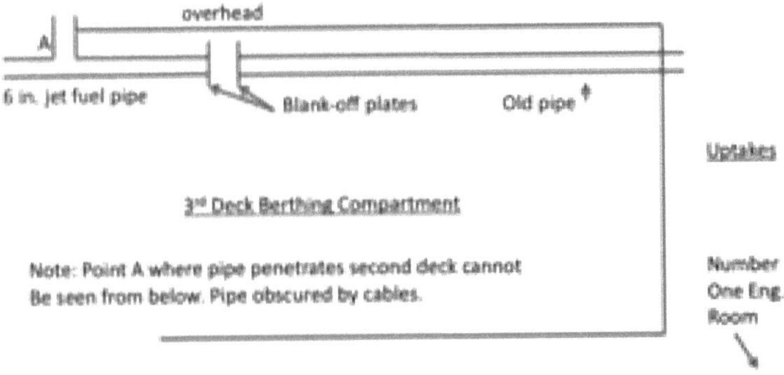

"Okay, tell me if I got this straight," Pete said. "Twelve years ago we put a safety modification into the fuel system. Jet fuel piping used to run through the uptakes above the engine rooms. That was considered to be a safety hazard. The piping was rerouted around the uptakes, but the drawings weren't updated, and the old piping wasn't removed. Our fuel guys had a problem with low pressure. They found that break in the pipe with the blank-off plates. It didn't match the diagrams, so they assumed that was the cause of low pressure. They reconnected the pipe back up the way the diagram showed. In doing so they created an opening for fuel to run into the uptakes, exactly what the safety mod tried to prevent. That right?"

"Right," Harry said. "Then First Class Petty Officer Griggs—and, Jesus, it hurts when an experienced petty officer screws up—started pumping early. And he didn't stop when we called the fire. He assumed it was the dumb engineers. Seven minutes after the fire was announced, you had the Air Boss check with his fuel guys. The aviation fuels officer called all the pump rooms. They told him they were not pumping, but Griggs lied and kept right on pumping. For forty minutes. We dumped a lot of jet fuel into the number one engine room."

"Our anonymous screw-off, stone sober, right, XO?" Harry shrugged.

Pete grabbed the cell phone and gave an update to Captain Barton.

"Right, Chief of Staff. But we are not out of the woods. The heat from the boilers has vaporized the jet fuel spill. It's billowing out of the smokestack. And how the hell long does Halon last? That damn space is not airtight. Oxygen could be building up in there right now. And the boilers are still hot enough to vaporize more fuel."

Pete hung up.

"Listening to you describe our situation to chief of staff," Harry said, "it occurred to me that we have a FAE in our smokestack."

FAE: fuel air explosive bombs. The navy and air force had built a few. Harry'd been on a test range when one was tested. It had flattened houses over a half acre. It knocked a massive hangar door off its tracks five miles from the detonation. The engine room and the uptakes were filled with vaporized fuel, the exact explosive in a FAE, and a hell of a lot more of it than had been packaged into that puny bomb.

Pete swiveled his chair and faced Harry.

"Last thing he said, Harry, 'Sometimes I wish you guys would have a normal problem. But you have to keep coming up with new and exotic ways to get in trouble.'"

Nothing to say to that, Harry thought.

"Okay to strike below, Cap'n? I'll be with Fred in Damage Control Central."

"Yeah, and one more thing. Chief of staff said he was sending a Commander Smedley out to work with Fred. He's the firefighting expert on the admiral's staff. He'll be here at 1300."

Harry saluted and left.

14

CAPTAIN PETE ADLER

That cellular phone was right there in front of him. He wanted to call Colleen. A lot of guys probably wanted to call a wife or a girlfriend—both? Some might even want to call their pop. But none of them had a phone. Pete was the CO and did. Using it for a personal reason felt wrong, like a sin against the navy.

A call to Colleen Riley Adler on one side of the coin, on the other…

He thought about the day. He thought about *the day* every day.

High school junior year was about over. He'd been in several classes with Colleen over the three years but never really paid any attention to her. She was a girl. He did notice that. Then that Thursday in May of 1958, he got a ride with Margo Hauptmann. She had a 1956 Ford convertible. They were driving away from the Catholic high school on Elm Street in St. Charles. The three girls in the car and Margo had three separate high-intensity conversations going on at once. They were on their planet. Pete sat in a corner of the rear seat, just happy to have a ride and not have to hitchhike for a change.

Colleen was walking along the side of Elm, three books in her left arm, the hem of her blue pleated uniform skirt dancing as she walked home. The afternoon sun pinned a gold barrette to the side of her just-above-the-shoulders brown hair. Wearing a short-sleeved white uniform blouse, carrying her blue sweater in the other hand, walking purposefully, she wore those saddle oxfords of hers with the funky fore and aft run of red and white, instead of the usual across-shoe pattern. She caught a lot of ribbing over those shoes.

They drove past her, and wham. Just, wham! It wasn't like Cupid nailed Pete with an arrow. He felt like he wanted to rip his chest open, show her his heart, and say, "There."

Married twenty-five years, going steady for thirty. He dialed.

She picked up.

"Colleen, we have a problem." "You okay?"

"Yes."

"A problem?"

"Yeah. We had a fuel spill and a fire. The fire's out, but we've still got a lot of fuel in wrong places. So we're not out of the woods. Anyway, I just wanted to give you a heads up."

"I'll call the ombudsman. She should know."

"No. Don't call anyone, not yet. If we need the ombudsman involved, I'll let you know. I…I just wanted to hear…to let you know. I'll keep you updated. Gotta go. Love you."

Pete hung up and stared at the phone. She didn't get hysterical. Didn't ask stupid questions. He had told himself the call was for Colleen. It wasn't.

All I did was give her something to worry—

No goddamned time for an examination of conscience.

The white smoke.

Pete went back out onto the catwalk, climbed the ladder, and put a finger in a trickle of jet fuel. He didn't know why, but he needed to do it. There didn't seem to be more of the liquid. There was that.

He went back into the pilothouse and called DC Central. "Okay, Fireball. Now we know what caused the problem. We know we pumped a lot of jet fuel into the uptakes. The uptakes run atop all four engine rooms, but we haven't had fuel spilling into the other ones, right?"

"Right. The other three engine rooms are fine. I had guys remove an access cover to the uptakes to check it out, but heavy fuel fumes spilled out and they shut it up again. We pumped a lot of fuel into the uptakes, but I think most of it ran down into the number one engine room."

"I'm worried the Halon will dissipate and the stuff will blow. If it's hot enough in there to vaporize the fuel, it's hot enough to set off an explosion. Lack of oxygen is probably all that's saving us. What can we do about that? There's no automatic system we can activate from outside the space, right? So if we're going to do something, we have to send people in? Is that right?"

"XO and I talked about this. We don't think we should send any people in there."

"So what the hell can we do? We just sit around with our thumbs up our butts and wait for this big-assed bomb we're sitting on to blow up?"

"Captain, we've got the number one engine room secured. The uptakes are a sealed-off space. We've got a problem, but it's boxed up in steel."

Think, Pete. Think. That's why they pay you the big bucks.

"You say something, Cap'n?"

"Fred, the boilers have to still be hot in number one because we're still boiling fuel off. The flow of vaporized fuel hasn't slowed. Look at your video camera. That stuff is still pouring out. What can we do to cool those boilers down more quickly?"

"We could—" "What?"

"Nah. I started talking before I really thought it through.

There's nothing to do but wait. Waiting's the right thing."

Pete hung up. Nothing to do. Wait. He wanted, needed to do something. He sensed that if he just sat and waited, the clock ticked catastrophe closer and closer. *Do something! Do something!* sounded in his head like his pop goading him. "Wait!"

"Wait for what, Cap'n?" the OOD asked.

Pete shook his head. He didn't want to admit he'd been talking to himself.

"I'm going back to the catwalk again to check the smokestack."

Pete charged out the door, stomped to the ladder welded to the stack, and climbed.

Five rivulets, each no wider than a pinky, trickled down. Above Pete, white clouds of vaporized fuel billowed. He put his hand on the side of the smokestack, his fingers splayed open. Little puddles of jet fuel filled the valleys formed by adjacent fingers.

Suddenly, he knew. He knew a massive explosion of vaporized fuel was imminent. He knew. He didn't know what would happen when it blew. The whole ship might vaporize. If the ammo magazines and five million gallons of ship and jet fuel triggered sympathetically, God only knew what would happen. It could trigger the big one. California could break off and sink.

Only one thing seemed sure: he'd never see Colleen again.

He felt as if he'd been kicked in the stomach, kneed in the balls, elbowed in the throat, and poked in the eye at the same time.

With his hand still pressed to the side of the stack, he recalled the navy recruiter office.

Riding home after Pete signed where the navy petty officer pointed a condemning finger, he asked Pop, "Why the navy?"

"You couldn't handle the army. Marines would never take you."

During the last phone call, Fred had started telling Pete something about cooling down the boilers. Fred stopped in midsentence.

Son of a bitch!

Back in the pilothouse, he picked up the phone to call Fred but stopped and put it back. He had to get his head straight. If he told Fireball he'd had a Vulcan mind meld with a molecule of jet fuel, Fred and the XO would put him in a straightjacket.

Cool, Pete. Be cool.

He dialed.

"Cap'n here, Fred. XO there?"

Harry picked up another phone. "Here, Cap'n."

"Good. Fred, when we talked before, you started telling me something we might do to cool the boilers down more quickly. You stopped talking. You stopped because you didn't want to give me any ideas. You didn't want me to order you to send people into number one. What was the idea you bit off?"

It was quiet. Fred probably had his hand over the mouthpiece.

"Fred, goddamn it, we don't have time for dicking around.

Talk to me."

"I'm here."

"Okay. My gut tells me this thing is getting ready to blow. I want to know what we can do to cool the boilers."

"There's only one thing, Cap'n," the XO said. "Trip the safety valves in number one. It would vent off the steam in a rush instead of trickling it out. But we'll probably lose the guys, and they might not be able to trip the safeties before they die in there."

"Got it, XO. But we have 3,500 people aboard. If the vaporized fuel blows up we could lose all of us and send the ship to the bottom. Get a team together and send them in there, and do it right now."

"Captain—"

"Don't argue. I understand the odds: 85 percent chance we'll kill them. Only 5 percent chance of tripping the vents. I'm just not as confident as Fred that our steel bulkheads will contain the explosion. I got it. I got it all, and it's all on me. Now get a goddamned team together. Send them in that space. Trip those friggin' safeties. Move!"

"Aye, aye."

The ship was turning.

"What the hell you doing, OOD?"

"We got a helo to land, Cap'n. I'm turning us into the wind."

Cool. Be cool. Admiral Warren's staff guy, Smedley.

"Okay. Good."

Pete climbed up onto his chair. He thought about the guys getting ready to go into number one. He wished like hell he could go with them. Sitting there on his chair, he worried about those men. If he were with them, he wouldn't be worried. He'd be cussing the dumb son of a bitch who ordered him in there while he, the order-giver, sat on his ass. The damned CO chair. Pete was beginning to hate the thing.

The ship had been heading north. Now the bow swung past the

naval air station and the San Diego skyline. They steadied, looking at Mexico. Out his window to port, an H-3 helicopter flew toward the *Marianas*.

The XO called on the walkie-talkie. "I got a team of six men. Almost ready to go. Lieutenant Zoll's leading them."

Zoll, a Kojak head stuck on a Dick Butkus body. "He fit through the scuttle?" Pete asked.

"He'll fit. He's giving instructions to the crew. They'll be going in, in one minute. Uh, Cap'n—"

"XO, I know. Send 'em in."

Pete hung up, looked left, and watched the approaching H-3 Sea King helicopter decelerate, edge over the flight deck, and start to descend. Wind from the rotors buffeted the window next to him. The chopper was some twenty feet above the deck and settling to land.

Two huge balls of fire blew out from the port side of the ship with a *whomp*. The explosion tilted the helo's rotor, tossed it right at Pete.

II

...THEN IT HIT THE FAN

15

COMMANDER HAROLD PENNINGTON III

A BAD FEELING CRAWLED OUT OF the pit of Commander Pennington's stomach, climbed through his throat, and sat sour on his tongue. He did not want to send his men into number one engine room. They'd die in there.

The XO stood by a watertight door in a passageway on the second deck. Fifteen yards aft of him, Lieutenant Gronk Zoll finished briefing his five-man team next to the scuttle leading down into number one engine room. The exec had argued with the captain. The CO had listened. Then he said, "Send them in."

Harry'd considered refusing. In the end, he'd said, "Aye, aye, sir." He felt crappy about considering refusal, crappy about not refusing. He felt as if maggots roiled over dead spots on the skin of his soul.

He should have closed the door but couldn't tear his eyes away from Gronk and his team. All of them wore long-sleeved shirts, leather gloves, and their oxygen breathing apparatus (OBA) masks. Gronk didn't have his gloves on, or the OBA. His eyes hit the exec like accusation.

"Close it," Gronk bellowed. "We're going in."

As soon as they opened the scuttle into number one, explosive vapors would boil up out of the engine room. They had planned to seal off both ends of the passageway to contain the fumes. Standing behind Harry was a reserve team of six men suited up like Gronk's, but not wearing their masks. Once the tab on the canister was pulled, it produced oxygen for twenty minutes. A sailor never activated his OBA until he needed it.

Harry began to shut the door. Gronk started pulling on his breathing mask.

Blam!

The scuttle to number one blew out of the deck. Harry saw a ball of fire explode from the escape trunk. Gronk toppled backward. He knocked his men over like bowling pins on a roll that earned a spare. The door ripped from the XO's hands and clanged back against the bulkhead. Hot, lung-searing smoke pushed him back against the wall.

Harry coughed. His eyes burned. Rushing wind sound filled his ears. He couldn't see Gronk or the men. He could see a spike of flame spouting out of the escape hatch and flattening against the overhead. All he could think was, *Get Gronk.* He took a step. Someone grabbed his arm. It was Chief Cooper, the leader of the backup team.

"Gronk."

"You gotta leave." The chief tried to pull Harry toward the ladder leading up a level. Harry tried to jerk free. The chief wasn't as big as Gronk, but he was big enough.

"Goddamn it, XO, get your useless ass outta here." The chief shoved the exec onto the ladder steps.

Harry climbed, opened the door, stumbled out onto the hangar bay, dogged the door behind him to keep the smoke and fumes contained below, and fell to his knees coughing. It felt as if he were coughing up handfuls of lung tissue. He hacked and spat and was surprised that there was no blood in the green-black slime glob. He wiped up his spit with his handkerchief, stood, and felt dizzy. He was near amidships. The cavernous hangar bay was practically empty, only a few pieces of yellow maintenance equipment tied down in the forward section.

No airplanes aboard. One thing going for us. Yeah, the only thing.

"General Quarters, General Quarters..."

As if by magic, people appeared and started running toward battle stations.

The door behind the XO opened. A cloud of smoke and fumes billowed out. He moved forward to get out of the noxious gas. A steady stream of pairs of men wearing breathing gear stomped out of the cloud of smoke. He started counting. Six, eight, ten, then two more. Chief Cooper supported Gronk with one hand and dogged the door behind him with the other.

Harry looked at the Gronk's red, blistered face, eyebrows gone. The big man grinned and then grimaced.

"Smilin' hurts," Gronk said. "Right now, hurtin's good." He didn't smile again, though.

Quack Fowler, the senior medical officer, with an enlisted hospital corpsman in tow, hustled toward the group. During battle stations, Doc Fowler operated a triage on the hangar bay.

Chief Cooper pulled off his mask, turned Gronk over to the doc, and started checking with the ten men who'd been in the passageway below. None of them were injured.

"Burns to the face," Quack said as he examined Gronk. He lifted the hands, studied both sides. "Burns to the hands."

Gronk coughed. "Sucked in a little smoke, Doc," he said.

Harry glanced at Chief Cooper. The chief finished checking the men's equipment; then he led them through the hatch back down to the second deck.

As Doc Fowler gave instructions to the medical technician, the XO unstrapped Gronk's breathing gear, put it on, and followed the chief's team.

16

CAPTAIN PETE ADLER

THE ROUGH DECK MATTING DUG into Pete's knees. Rotor buffeting threatened to blast in the bridge windows behind him. The noise quit, suddenly, replaced by stunning silence, a sound black hole. Pete jumped up, looked out. No helo. Inside, bodies covered the deck, some prone, most on hands and knees.

Only the helmsman stood, eyes and mouth open wide. "Where's the helo?"

"Went off the bow and just dropped out of sight." The helmsman added, "Cap'n."

In the shadow under the bow. Close!

"Hard left rudder!"

There wasn't time to think which might be the better direction to turn. If the helo made it through the near collision with the island, if they ditched, only to get run over—

The helmsman spun the wheel with vigor, the way he was supposed to respond to a "hard" rudder command, but the bow plowed straight ahead.

Only going ten knots. Takes time for the rudder to bite. Shit. Number one engine was shut down.

A dragging number one propeller would slow turns to the left.

"Port engine back full!"

Usually, after ordering "reverse the propellers," there was a delay of several seconds before it could be felt on the bridge. But not then. It happened quickly. Pete felt the reversed propellers thrashing the sea and juddering through the deck. The ship was on fire, and the engineering crew was ready to jump on any order from the bridge.

The bow started moving, then moving good. Pete let out his held breath, ordered all engines ahead again, and hurried to the starboard side. *Jesus.* The ditched bird was close, the rotors still turning. He hoped like hell the ship's wake wouldn't swamp the helo.

The ship was through about sixty degrees of turn.

"Shift your rudder to hard right." They'd missed them with the bow. Then Pete had to stop the stern from swinging onto them. The dragging propeller should help the turn to starboard.

"Captain," the OOD said. "DC Central says we need to go to General Quarters."

"Set GQ." Pete hollered at the window. He didn't take his eyes off the bow. *Turn!* He hoped like hell he reversed soon enough to save the helo from the carrier's ass-end. The bow started coming back right. Pete glanced aft. The stern stopped swinging toward the helo.

Phew. Son of a bitch!

He spent a half second thinking how close a joyous "son of a bitch" and a catastrophic "oh shit" could be.

"All engines stop." He thought about ordering the launch of a boat to rescue the helo crew, but first—

He called DC Central.

"Fire's burning along the length of the uptakes and in number one," Fireball said. "Lotsa smoke and fumes to deal with in the aft half of the ship. GQ will help contain the fire and smoke."

"When number one blew, it almost shoved the helo bringing Smedley into the island," he told Fred. "It's in the water. I'm stopped. I want to try to launch a boat and get the crew."

He was going to ask about Zoll and his men they—he—had sent into number one. He wanted to ask about the XO.

Count bodies later.

"General Quarters, General Quarters. All hands man your battle stations. Condition Zebra will be set in five minutes," the bosun said into his microphone.

Pete took the mic from him and waited for the *gong, gong, gong* to stop. "This is the captain. We have a helo in the water. We need to launch a boat to pick the crew up. Deck Officer, call the captain on the bridge."

Pete handed the mic back. The OOD stood in front of the helmsman. Their eyes met. "Call the admiral's chief of staff on that cellular phone. Let me know when he's on the line."

The ditched chopper's rotors had stopped. It listed to port, taking on water. The ship was headed west. Winds were from the south. When the boat launched, he wanted to be on a westerly heading, just like they were then, so the carrier would shield the boat and helo from wind and waves. He planned to drive the carrier in a circle around the helo and get closer to it.

"Engines ahead two-thirds." His voice surprised him. He hadn't hollered.

The phone rang. The Air Boss. "Captain, got a call from the Sea King pilot on emergency radio. Their crewman was knocked out when they maneuvered to miss us."

"Okay, Boss. Tell them we're putting a boat in the water. I'm sending the lance corporal to you. Give him one of your handheld emergency radios."

Pete turned to look for him, but Lance Corporal Solomon was already out the door.

The phone rang. DC Central. "The space in front of number one is an ammo magazine," Fred said. "Bulkhead is getting hot. We may have to flood the space."

A lot of crap tried to shove its way into Pete's brain.

How many guys have I killed so far? Life-and-death choices over here, choices over there, still more in other places.

Pete couldn't say where the hell the thought came from, but he loved the shit out of being in the middle of it.

"You there, Captain?"

"Yeah. Tell them to take any rockets, flares, anything that's extra touchy, and throw it all over the side. The rest of the stuff, move it away from the heat. Spray the bulkhead with a fire hose. See if that works. If any of you think it needs to be flooded, flood it."

Pete slammed the phone down.

The OOD said, "The chief of staff, Captain." He held out the cellular handset.

Pete snatched the phone. "Abner, it blew. Good news is we're still afloat."

Pete described the fire locations and severity and reported the near helicopter crash.

"I'll put a helicopter squadron on alert here at the air station.

Holler with what you need."

"Launch a medevac. There's at least one injured on that bird in the water."

Pete slammed the cellular down. The phone rang. He jerked it up.

The deck officer said, "Captain, I can get a boat in the water in about seven minutes."

"You got four and a half!" Phone slam.

17

CAPTAIN PETE ADLER

PETE WAS ON THE STARBOARD side of the pilothouse, watching the helo.

From behind him a voice said, "Cap'n." It was Harry!

Son of a bitch! He was alive.

Thanks, God, for not letting me kill his ass.

A lump clogged Pete's throat. Harry's face was blackened with soot, his khakis soaked, his shoes meringue-frosted with firefighting foam.

Pete muscled the baseball-sized lump of emotion down his throat. "Clean Harry, you look like shit."

"But I feel pretty." Dirty Clean Harry grinned. "Oh so pretty."

Pete snapped from wanting to cry to wanting to laugh like a lunatic. More throat muscling rising lumps back down.

The XO had lost his walkie-talkie. Pete gave him his and told him to call the deck officer and get the damned boat in the water.

Harry took the talkie, walked aft a few paces, and pressed the mic. "Deck Officer, XO..."

Pete went back to driving the ship. He'd decided on a new game plan. They'd launch the boat on a southerly heading. Once the boat crew had rescued the people from the helo, he'd use the ship to block the wind. Pete was afraid if he broadsided the carrier to the stiff breeze, the way he'd originally planned, it could push the ship onto the floating helo. There were a lot of ways the rescue could be screwed up. *Just keep your head outta your ass, Pete. Keep thinking.*

Lance Corporal Solomon burst in the door and handed him a radio and another walkie-talkie. Pete clipped the talkie to his belt and keyed the radio.

"Sea King, this is Birdfarm. Give me the number and condition of souls aboard."

"This is Sea King, Birdfarm. Four souls," the pilot responded. "Crewman banged his head, cracked his helmet. He's unconscious. Breathing. Rest of us are good."

"Okay, Sea King, we have a quack standing by on our hangar bay. Boat's about to launch."

The XO was done talking. Pete sent him down to the hangar bay to supervise the helo rescue. As soon as Harry left, Pete wished he'd asked him about the men he'd ordered into number one.

Just drive the boat, Pete. See if you can keep from screwing up the helo rescue.

Pete thought about keeping the conn, the responsibility for driving the ship. Helmsmen were trained to only respond to the conning officer. Even the captain announced, "This is the captain. I have the conn."

But he needed to find out about the fire too. He couldn't do it all himself. He had good people.

"Officer of the Deck." Pete beckoned, come.

Lieutenant Commander Wiley was the OOD for General Quarters. Pete explained to him about the wind, about positioning the carrier for the boat and survivors recovery.

"Got it, Wiles?" "Yes, sir."

"This is the captain. The officer of the deck has the conn." Pete immediately snatched up the phone and dialed DC Central. A small slice of his brain listened to the helmsman acknowledging the change of conning officer.

"Central." It was Fred. "Status."

"Cap'n. Okay. Fires raging in the uptakes. Second deck above number one is sealed off. I have teams searching areas adjacent to the uptakes to see if the heat is torching off secondary fires."

"Other three engine rooms?" "Good."

"Electricity? Fire main pressure?" "Good and good."

Pete slammed the phone down.

He'd been so sure the ship would be blown apart. Maybe Fireball Fred had been right. Maybe their problem was contained in a steel box. Maybe they'd get out of this without too much damage.

Maybe.

He walked to the starboard side, checked on the rescue, and asked Medina for the fire log.

18

FIRE LOG

FIRE LOG (PO3 MEDINA)

1100: Fire in number one engine room announced. 1101: Slowed from twenty-two to ten knots.

1102: Fuel leak in number one engine room. Burning fuel running down sides of boilers. Shut down boilers. Space abandoned. Halon system activated.

1103: DC Central manned and ready.

1105: CO called DC Central to report white smoke from stack. Chief engineer said white smoke was steam.

1106: Air Boss ensured no jet fuel being pumped. 1107: XO reported no injuries to number one engine room crew. Deck above number one not hot. Halon appears to have extinguished fire. Flight operations pushed back two hours.

1111: CO called Vice Admiral Warren's chief of staff on cellular phone with Sitrep.

1115: This item copied from DC Central log. Chief engineer called Commander Smedley on Admiral Warren's staff via radio phone-patch. Ship's diagrams show aviation fuel lines running through uptakes above number one engine room. Smedley said those aviation fuel lines were removed twelve years ago. Ship's diagrams not updated.

1120: Ship steaming back and forth ten to twenty miles from North Island Naval Air Station.

1121: Captain left pilothouse to check smokestack. 1124: Captain reported smelling jet fuel from catwalk below smokestack. Informed DC Central and XO. Ordered Air Boss to have aviation fuel pump rooms inspected. Ordered aviation fuels officer to the pilothouse.

1140: Discovered that aft aviation fuel pump room had been pumping fuel for forty minutes. Fuel pumping operations secured. Petty officer in charge of the pump room violated standard procedure by activating pumps too soon and disobeyed a direct order to cease pumping.

1200. Chief engineer determined the source of the fuel leak into the uptakes and the cause of the fire. Drawing attached to last page of the log book.

1230: Halon continues to suppress fire in number one engine room.

1302: Observation from OOD: "At 1300, I was standing in front of the helmsman, looking to starboard, clearing the area. After we landed an H-3 helicopter, I intended turning that direction. Suddenly I saw two huge fireballs rise from approximately amidships. Obviously number one engine room blew up. From the size of those fireballs, I thought the ship would break in half. Thank you, God, it didn't. The captain hollered, "Hit the deck!" It was a tone of voice you couldn't ignore. I hit the deck.

1302: General Quarters called to contain fires raging in the uptakes, involving a third of the length of the ship.

1303: Observation from PO3 Medina. I was standing on the port side of the pilothouse. Two bells were being struck. A helicopter approached to land on the flight deck. The chopper was about twenty feet in the air, everything going normal. All of a sudden, I saw two fireballs appear off the port side, each as big as the helo. The helo went from level to looking like it was going to fly right into the pilothouse. I watched the rotor blades coming at me. I thought they were going to chop my head off. The captain hollered, "Hit the deck!" I did.

1305: From DC Central. Fuel vapors in number one engine room blew up. Gases from explosion and fire vented from number one engine room via ventilation ducting. Two large fireballs appeared on each side of the ship near midship.

1307: From OOD. At 1300, fireballs, each approximate size of Sea King helicopter, appeared off starboard and port sides. Fireballs on port side almost forced a landing helo into the island, but the pilot managed to regain control. Helo damaged by the explosion, and pilot ditched. The captain maneuvered the ship to avoid running over the floating helo.

1310: Bulkhead between number one engine room and magazine hot. Sensitive ammo (rockets, flares) jettisoned. Bulkhead sprayed with fire hose.

1312: Four men rescued from helo by ship's boat. One helo crewman sustained a head injury.

1314: Sea King helicopter sank.

1315: Boat delivered rescued crewmen to hangar bay and medical triage station.

19

COMMANDER HAROLD PENNINGTON III

HARRY WAS STANDING IN THE hangar bay next to Quack Fowler looking out onto the aft aircraft elevator and at the motor whaleboat approaching with the four rescuees. If he walked out onto the elevator he'd have to have a life preserver. He considered busting the policy. He was the XO after all. Nobody would say anything to him, but he decided there'd been plenty of rule violations that day. He watched from the hangar.

The CO had positioned the ship to shelter the boat from the wind and wind-driven chop. Still, the tiny boat bounced up and down in what looked like ripples. The deck officer had the wheeled boat crane positioned on the elevator. He planned to hoist the boat out of the water with the passengers still inside. Trying to get the head injury aboard any other way would probably hurt the kid even more.

Attaching hoisting gear to a bobbing boat had injured and killed plenty of sailors over the years. If it began to look like a goat rope, Harry was going out onto the elevator, life jacket or not. The deck officer was Paul Molsby. His sailors knew what they were doing. They were careful and one of the boat crew shielded the injured man with his own body. Paul stood on the edge of the elevator, gauged the wave action, and gave the "up" signal.

The boat came out of the water, swung over the elevator, and settled onto the boat trailer.

Paul saw the XO watching him. Paul grinned. "Walk in the park, XO," he hollered over the crane's diesel clatter.

"Real close to satisfactory work, Paul," Harry said. "Now quit screwing around. Get that boat into the hangar so Quack can check out his patient."

The hangar deck crewman pulled the boat trailer onto the hangar and stopped. Quack Fowler climbed into the boat and checked out the injured man.

Quack looked over the gunwale. "Kid's responsive, XO. He'll be okay."

The boat crew strapped the injured sailor into a wire basket stretcher and then lowered him to the deck with a forklift. Four men grabbed corners of the stretcher and headed for sickbay.

Harry called the CO on the walkie-talkie and reported the condition of the helo crewman.

"What about Zoll, and his men? Are they...?"

"No, no. They're okay, Cap'n." *Shit. Shoulda told him.* "Zoll has burns to his face and hands. Quack says it'll take some time, but he'll recover. Plus we have a few smoke inhalation cases." Harry condensed the tale of the explosion at the escape scuttle and disconnected.

The deck crew shut down the diesel engine of the boat hoist. In the abrupt onset of silence, Harry heard two people arguing.

Just forward of the aircraft elevator, one of the helo crewmen shouted at a chief petty officer from the safety department.

"Knock it off, you two," the XO said. "What's going on, Chief?"

Chief Mills was a six-footer, 180 or so, the same height and build as the helo crewman.

"XO, the lieutenant here doesn't want to give a urine sample.

We have to collect one after a crash."

"I need a medicinal brandy, man, after what I been through."
"The procedure is we get the sample, you write your statement, and then if the doc prescribes it, brandy." "Balls. I—"

"What's your name, Lieutenant?"

"Littlejohn, sir. I was the copilot."

"The safety officer took the pilot to get his sample and statement," the chief said. "The LT doesn't want to cooperate. He's probably got drugs in his system, XO."

"You gonna come up clean, Littlejohn?" "I'm not a goddamned doper."

"Here's what you're going to do, Chief," Harry said. "Take him to sick bay. Get a urine sample, get him a brandy, and then get his statement. In that order." Harry turned to the copilot. "Urine sample, brandy, statement. Got it?"

"This way, sir," the chief said to the lieutenant.

"Oh, Chief," the XO said. "Ask the safety officer to call me when the statements are done. Must have been a hell of ride."

"It was that, XO," Littlejohn said.

The fire.

When they were picking up the boat on the starboard side, the ship stopped. The wind had been from port. Thick black smoke poured from the smokestack and the wind carried it into view from the hangar. Now the ship was steaming at probably ten knots. No smoke was visible out the opening for the aircraft elevator. No other evidence of the fire was visible from the hangar.

Harry crossed to port and descended a level. Smoke and fumes filled the passageway, but the crew had set up ventilation blowers. The air was breathable with a little chewing.

He went on to Damage Control Central.

Fred sat at his desk with his yeoman Sanchez next to him.

Harry took the chair on the other side of Fred.

Fred barked into his walkie-talkie, "Team leaders, report."

Six teams reported battling secondary fires on the second and third decks in spaces adjacent to the uptakes. Storage rooms with electronic parts in cardboard and paper packing, bedding, admin storage areas, all were burning.

"Central, Team One. Be advised we're going through a potload of OBA canisters."

"Central, Team Five. Roger the canisters, and we're going through firefighting foam pretty fast too. We're going to run out before this is over."

Fred acknowledged.

"I'll call Smedley's office back on the beach," Fred said to the XO. "They'll scramble us up the supplies."

"Phone the captain. Ask him to call the chief of staff on the cellular. Let's lean on the big guns."

Fred called the captain, told him about the secondary fires, ticked off the supplies they needed, and slammed the phone down.

Fred looked at the XO with a sheepish grin. "Oops. Please and thank you, maybe?"

"Please and thank yous later. Show me on the diagram where these secondary fires are."

They walked to the layout of the ship's compartments etched onto four-by-eight-foot sheets of Plexiglas. Fred pointed to the affected area.

Harry wrote in his pocket-sized notebook and snapped it shut.

"You got enough people to fight these new fires, Fred?" "So far."

"Okay. I'm going to see Quack and check on injuries. Give the captain and me a report every fifteen minutes. Have Sanchez do it if you get tied up."

20

PETTY OFFICER SECOND CLASS SAMANTHA INSKO

Twenty-three-year-old Samantha Insko sat on a cruise-box in the line shack off the starboard side forward and under the flight deck, leaning back against the bulkhead. The fifteen sailors in her crew sprawled on the deck, some asleep, some reading paperbacks. Two had comic books. Not one of her guys was twenty, although Carrot, one of the comic-book guys, would be next month. When newbies checked in to the squadron, most of them wound up in the line division, where they worked much as knights' pages had in the olden days, doing the most basic maintenance chores, such as helping a pilot launch on a mission or securing the plane after a flight. Her guys liked waiting. It beat the heck out of working on the flight deck, with the noise, the danger of being sucked down an intake, the danger of being blown over the side by jet blast, walking with a dozen greasy aircraft tie-down chains draped over their shoulders. She hated waiting.

Her mind went back to Lemoore, California, and to her boyfriend, Arnold. Until she met him, she thought she might just stay in the navy for twenty years. But he stirred feelings she'd frozen out of her heart long ago. After dating Arnold for nine months, the change he brought into her outlook, her approach to life, and maybe into her soul amazed her anew each day.

During her freshman year of high school, she'd set a course for her life to follow. Many of her female classmates would have killed for the attention the jocks aimed at her, but to Samantha, that slobbering-at-the-mouth lust turned her off more than green snot trickling out of their noses would have. Actually, that would have worked too. She'd pushed back, not like the other girls, about one-third serious and two-thirds worried they'd quit coming around. Her pushback wasn't physical, or even vocal. She'd scan them up and down wanting the look on her face to tell them they were scum, the lowest kind of trash. More than once she'd seen a pest turn away and check that his zipper was up. They'd called her IBLI, Ice Bitch Lezzie Insko.

Samantha focused on her studies and figured out how to nail Bs. She didn't want an A. They drew attention, and she didn't want that from teachers or classmates of either gender. The lezzie thing rankled. Those pea-brained cesspools of testosterone seemed to think that if any female declined their obvious manly attributes, said female must be a lesbian.

She poured herself into basketball and soccer. On field or court, she could score but had a real talent for feeding a teammate in the instant she found an opening. Her coaches encouraged her to socialize with the team, but she rejected the notion that camaraderie was essential for optimum team performance. In her senior year, her Bobcat team lost the state championship basketball game to five female trees.

The judo club was her only other high school activity. Mr. Kramer, the physics teacher, taught judo and sponsored the club. He was the only one, teacher or student, from her high school years she remembered fondly. He respected her for her ability, not because she had "legs up to here," Barbie boobs, and looked like a Farrah Fawcett with short hair who never smiled.

Mr. Kramer.

Naval Air Station Lemoore, her home base, sprawled over several thousand acres on the west side of the San Joaquin Valley. The town of Lemoore was seven miles east. Samantha volunteered to assist with coaching the girl's high school basketball team, the Tigers. That's how she met Arnold. After an early season game, a lanky six-foot-two guy sauntered up to her.

"Tigers'r four and oh." His head twitched in what Samantha considered to be a gesture of admiration, maybe. "Ma'am." He tipped his white cowboy hat and ambled away.

A girl giggled behind her. It was Alison, a junior on the team, a forward.

"My uncle Arnold. Kinda cute, isn't he?"

Enough of this reminiscing crap.

The ship's announcing system had told them the carrier was on fire. GQ told them the fire was serious. The next thing they'd know, probably, was that the fire was out and it was time to get back to work.

God, she hated waiting. She got up, careful to not bang her head on the low overhead. She was five nine, and the huge I-beams supporting the flight deck had already given her some knots. Picking up the phone, she dialed maintenance control.

"Petty Officer Insko here, Chief. Has the ship asked for any help fighting the fire?"

"Nobody's called or come here. We're not going to be flying today, maybe not tomorrow either. If you want, you can go to the hangar bay and ask. Just make sure you leave two guys in the line shack and they know how to get in touch with you."

"Carrot," Samantha said as she hung up. "You're in charge here. Champ, Young, you two come with me. We're going to see if the Turkey needs some help fighting their fire."

Champ got up without a word.

"Take Elsworth, why don't you?" Young whined. Elsworth had joined the squadron a week ago and therefore rated getting all the crap details.

Samantha wasn't going to leave Young there for Carrot to try to handle. Carrot was okay, a bit of a wimp, but okay. Young was *the* major pain in the ass in the crew. She didn't say anything but stood looking down at him lying on his back.

Young's mouth mumbled F-droppings, but he pushed himself up. Samantha turned and led the way out of the shack, across the flight deck, into the island, and down to the hangar bay.

21

COLLEEN

THE THINGS SHE HAD TO do tugged at Colleen. They were out of Kotex and Kleenex and low on toilet paper again. Socks—it was harder to keep the girls in socks than it was to keep the paper products pantry stocked. White blouses, clothes the high school girls would wear—*arrgh,* tennis shoes. Full-time job number one, shopping for the girls. Groceries, the house, *Marianas* officers' wives' club, meeting with the ombudsmen.

There was no point in counting her full-time jobs. She had to take advantage of shopping windows of opportunity.

The phone pulled at her harder, though. After getting the call from Pete about the fuel leak, leaving the telephone was out of the question. He would have his hands full. She knew that. Still, she wanted, needed him to call again. She rubbed her hand over her heart.

Call!

Colleen sat on the sofa in the small sunroom at the rear of the house, feet up on the cushioned hassock, *Alaska* open on her lap. She and Pete both enjoyed James Michener, and they always bought his latest book, even if birthday, anniversary, or holiday gift could not be used as the excuse for spending the money on a new hardback. But her mind was too much with Pete to permit an excursion to the forty-ninth state.

"He's busy," she said aloud to her empty house, and stood up.

Through the open blinds, the backyard Birds of Paradise peeked up above the windowsill. None of the neighbor kids were playing on the large, grassy well-shaded common area. It would have been nice to see another living soul.

It was 2:30, 1430. Her mind did that. It registered civilian time and immediately translated it to military. At 1500 she had to leave to pick up her three grade-schoolers from their summer program at Sacred Heart in Coronado. The two high school girls were at the beach on base. *Come home!* The oldest, Marci, only had a learner's permit. She couldn't pick up the girls, but she could answer the phone. Colleen hated the thought of even walking to a neighbor's house to ask for help.

At that moment the phone was her connection to heaven, to earth, to everything that was not her girls. Pete had asked her to keep the information about the fire to herself.

Ring! Please?

A knock at the back screen door startled her. The Adlers lived in Quarters J, one of a handful of senior officer houses, occupying a corner of land between BOQ buildings and the airfield on Naval Air Station North Island. An admiral, four navy captains, and the base XO lived in houses close to Quarters J. The location on the base and the neighbors made it the nicest place they'd ever lived.

A neighbor, Sally Hammond, stood on the back porch in her tennis outfit.

"Come in, Sally."

Sally frowned wrinkles into her forehead under the white sweatband corralling her blonde hair.

"Colleen, I just got back from tennis, and I saw the Turkey steaming back and forth a couple of miles off the beach. She was supposed to be going out to sea today, right?"

Pete's ship was the USS *Marianas*, named after the World War II carrier battle nicknamed the Marianas Turkey Shoot. Inevitably, navy men purloined the battle nickname and applied just the fowl part to the ship. *Marianas* sailors hated for their ship to be called Turkey. Bar fights erupted regularly over the slight.

"Sorry," Sally said.

"Come in, Sally."

"No, thanks. I can't. I just wanted to mention seeing the *Marianas.* Is everything okay with the ship, with Pete?"

Colleen knew that Sally saw something on her face. She wrestled with whether to tell her.

A helo *whop, whopped* down the runway, heading south. Another, then a third followed. The engine and rotor noises rattled the windows.

Colleen saw the concern and fear on Sally's face. She figured it mirrored her own.

Inside, the kitchen phone rang.

Colleen stood in the doorway, turned, and looked at the wallphone, but couldn't make her legs carry her toward it. Sally moved Colleen aside and stepped past her, and the screen door slammed, startling them both. Sally led the way, lifted the handset, and handed it to Colleen.

"Hello." Colleen's voice squeaked.

22

CAPTAIN PETE ADLER

FIREBALL CALLED WITH HIS SHOPPING list. Pete relayed it to the chief of staff, Abner Barton.

The XO called on the walkie-talkie with an injury report. "Fifteen cases of smoke inhalation. The helo crewman has a concussion, but he's alert, responsive. Gronk has burns to face and hands. We need to get him to the naval hospital. Any word on when the medevac helos arrive?"

Pete glanced out the window toward the naval air station. "I don't see anything coming yet, but it shouldn't be long. Chief of staff told me he'd be scrambling a medevac helo plus at least four more with OBA canisters."

"We'll put our medevacs into the supply helos for the return trip. I'll get the ops officer to coordinate."

Pete slipped the talkie back onto his belt and climbed up onto his chair.

What the hell kind of beast from hell will bite us on the ass next? Something sure as hell will.

The helos. They'd be managing a lot of helos on an airport used to handling lots of jets. On the ship he commanded prior to coming to *Marianas,* they were conducting a major exercise with the flight deck filled with helos. Marines filed up from below the flight deck and onto the choppers, which lifted off and hauled the jarheads ashore to assault exercise objectives. Things were going fine, and then one of the helos developed a system failure. There was a single spot on the flight deck that could accommodate a spare aircraft. They used it. The problem was that the flight deck crew was not used to operating helos from that spot. The flight deck was packed with choppers, all rotors turning, and a sailor had walked into the tail rotor of the aircraft on the spare spot and been decapitated. Flight decks were dangerous as hell, but routine and training managed the hazard to a tolerable level.

Pete hopped down. He had to talk to the Air Boss. The Boss needed to make sure his guys were ready to handle a dense pack of rotor aircraft on the flight deck.

The phone rang. Fireball reported that they were running out of one more thing: D-cell flashlight batteries. The power was off in the areas where they were fighting the fires, which was now a good portion of the aft half of the ship below the hangar. Pete told the Gator to call Captain Barton on the cellular with the additional requirement, and he, with Solomon on his heels, charged out the door, along the catwalk, and into the control tower.

The Air Boss sat on a chair, much like Pete's on the bridge. His windows gave him a good view of the flight deck and the airspace to the carrier's port side.

"We're going to have a potload of helos to deal with shortly, Boss," Pete said. "The guys are used to watching out for jet exhaust and intakes. Now the danger is tail rotors."

"We've talked about it, Cap'n," the Boss said. "I've got a flight deck chief who served on an amphib flight deck. He said they packed the helos pretty closely. Twelve feet of main rotor to tail rotor clearance is what they used."

"Boss, this isn't an amphib op, where we're transporting a bunch of jarheads ashore as quickly as we can. The amphibs practice specifically for that purpose. We are not used to operating helos like that. We'll be using forklifts to unload pallets of supplies."

"Okay. We'll put more distance between—"

"No, not just more distance. Designate three specific spots on the flight deck to land helos. Three. Designate a couple of guys at each spot to be guides and to direct people and fork lifts around tail rotors."

"Sorry, Cap'n, I shoulda thought of that."

"Boss, not one of us knows enough to get us through this.

Together, though, we know some stuff."

A small shiny helo buzzed close aboard the port side of ship, probably 300 feet above the water.

"What the hell is that?" Pete asked.

The Boss grabbed his binocs. "TV-7 news chopper."

"Call him on emergency. Tell him to stay five miles away from us. Tell him if he endangers any of the aircraft coming to help us, I will personally hunt down the pilot when this is over, and I will rip his throat out."

"You…you really want me to say that on the radio, Cap'n?" the Boss asked.

"Get that son of a bitch out of our airspace, Boss. If you don't, I'll get the Marines to shoot it down." Pete turned around. "Your buds like some target practice, Solomon?"

"Whatever you say, Captain."

The Boss snatched up a microphone, flipped a switch on a panel in the overhead above him. He keyed the mic. "News helicopter eight miles west of Naval Air Station North Island operating near the USS *Marianas*, you are interfering with emergency operations."

Pete charged out of the control tower and back to the pilothouse. He made a call to the chief of staff. Then he called Colleen.

"It's Pete. Our fuel spill, it caught fire. We've got fifteen, no, seventeen injuries. We're medevacing all of them to Balboa Naval Hospital."

"Are you okay, Pete?"

"I haven't killed anybody." "Pete."

"I—"

"I love you too, Pete. What do you need me to do?"

He couldn't say anything for a moment. "Okay, I talked to Admiral Warren's chief of staff. Abner's going to get Chaplain Dawson involved. And it's time for you to call the senior ombudsman.

The fire's been burning for an hour and a half. We're still a ways from getting the sucker under control. That's how it stands. Oh, and we've had a news helicopter buzz over us. It's probably already on the news."

"I know Chaplain Dawson. I have his number." Pete could hear rotor noise from her end.

"Pete, helos, a lot of them are taking off. For you?" Another helo took off, and another.

"The helicopters are bringing us firefighting supplies. We're using ours up pretty quickly."

"Pete."

"I won't tell you it's not serious. But the crew is good, they know what they're doing. I just thank great God in heaven I set us on fire close to the beach," Pete said. "Sorry, Colleen."

He hung up.

23

COMMANDER HAROLD PENNINGTON III

HARRY ENTERED THE HANGAR BAY from the port side and dogged the watertight door behind him. He unstrapped and took off his OBA.

Chief Cooper had his team of ten men seated on the deck in a circle. Quack Fowler had treated a couple of cases of dehydration. He insisted that Fireball order the firefighting teams to rotate breaks and get plenty of liquids. Hydration stations had been set up on the hangar bay for the purpose. Harry walked over to the chief.

"Your guys doing okay?"

"Yeah, XO. We're about ready to go back at it again."

"I just toured the third deck. Secondary fires going everywhere on the starboard side, but I saw teams dealing with each one of them. We're getting a handle on it."

The chief rapped his head. "Goddamnit, XO. You jinxed us." The chief's walkie-talkie crackled.

The chief responded, listened, and glared at the XO.

"DC Central just told me we got fires on the 01, 02, and 03 levels and that I need to get my ass up there."

"More secondary fires? How the hell are secondaries torching off up there? Along where the smokestack rises, maybe?"

"Don't know, XO. I gotta look, but if it's significant, we're gonna need people. We should muster up some training squadron pukes. Have them stand by here on the hangar."

"Shore duty pukes reporting for duty, Chief." Harry spun around.

Jesus!

The woman looked like a Barbie doll. Built. *Sailors shouldn't look like that in dungarees.* She did have short hair, but Harry's eyes weren't much interested in the coiffure.

Chief Cooper recovered first. "The hell you know about fighting fires?"

"I've been to plenty of schools," the girl said. "I know how to use a hose, how to use firefighting foam. I know how to use an OBA. You want help or not, Chief?"

"Your mouth's hanging open, XO," the chief said.

Harry clamped his mouth shut. He hoped the smudges on his face covered his blush.

"Chief Cooper." He stuck out a paw toward the girl.

She shook. "Petty Officer Insko. From the A-7 training squadron."

"Is it just you three?" The chief gestured at the two sailors behind Insko.

"How many do you need?" "Two dozen."

Petty Officer Insko sent one of her sailors to summon men from her squadron. The chief ordered five of his men to roust up extra OBAs.

"XO," the chief said. "You want to come with me to check the upper levels?"

Harry closed his mouth again. The chief smirked at him.

The two of them walked forward and climbed port-side-of-the-ship ladders to the 03 level. They crossed to starboard just aft of the admiral's quarters. The passageway was filled with smoke and choking fumes. They both donned OBA masks and pulled the tabs. Harry followed the chief to just outside Pete's inport cabin. The smoke and fumes were intense here. The chief looked up and pointed. Cables ran throughout the ship in racks welded to the overheads. Electrical and communication cables were bunched tightly above them. The smoke and fumes were coming from the cables.

Harry recalled some trouble in the past with flammable wiring insulation in navy jets. Did they have that same issue on the *Marianas*?

The hits keep on coming!

24

FIRE LOG, PAGE 19

1320: Lost steering. Rudder control cables passing through uptakes burned through. Control shifted to backup cables on port side.

1330: Operations officer coordinated helicopter resupply of firefighting supplies.

1331: News helicopter warned to evacuate area.

1333: Captain called Mrs. Adler to activate ombudsman support.

1345: A helicopter landed to evacuate smoke inhalation and burn victims to Balboa Naval Hospital. Helo transported five.

1347: Resupply helos arrive. Remaining medevac cases transported in empty supply helos.

1401: Captain called chief of staff to report status. Not under control, but fires in uptakes and number one engine room contained.

1405: Secondary fires reported throughout aft starboard

section of the ship on the second and third decks. Additional firefighting teams deployed.

1415: Captain initiated fifteen-minute status reports to chief of staff. Promised no more rosy forecasts until they had the "bastard whipped."

1430: Smoldering bedding in berthing compartments and fire in storage rooms on second and third deck. Teams deployed to all fire sites.

Consumption of firefighting supplies continues at high rate. Resupply keeping pace, barely.

1445: Fires on second and third decks 20 percent contained.

1555: Fires reported from 01 through 03 levels. Fires traveling up cable runs apparent source. Electrical power secured through major portions of starboard side of the ship because of cable fires. Consumption of D-cell flashlight batteries a rising concern. Additional firefighting teams formed from training squadron personnel.

1600: XO called Rear Admiral Miller's office. No officers present. Left message and cellular phone number.

25

CAPTAIN ABNER BARTON

THE CHIEF OF STAFF HUNG up the phone, left his office, took three steps to the admiral's door, knocked twice, and went in.

Vice Admiral Warren was seated behind his gleaming mahogany desk, a pencil in hand, looking down at a sheet of paper. His speechwriter, Chief Petty Officer Nora Emerson, stood behind the desk to the admiral's right.

The admiral looked up and his eyes hit Abner the way they always did, like lasers boring into a man's soul, seeking signs of mendacity. Those blue eyes, like they always did, reminded him of flying over Alaska and peering down into cracks in glaciers. It had been five years ago. He'd been in an F-14 Tomcat, and he'd launched from the USS *Marianas*. The flight over those glaciers and with the view into the incredible pure and clean blue in the cracks of dirt and rock-befouled glacier was his most cherished memory of all the things he'd been privileged to see from a fighter-plane cockpit.

"How's the *Marianas* doing?" the admiral asked. "I'll come back later, sir," Chief Emerson said.

She picked up the speech, and Abner watched the flat-chested, short, black-haired, cleft-chinned, plain of face, professional as hell chief stride to the door. It was the cleft chin that earned her the nickname Butt Ugly, which she wasn't, which had no bearing on the matter of whether the nickname would stick to her or not. None of the sailors who used the nickname would ever let her hear them using it. They knew they'd get their vocal cords ripped out. The door closed.

"Okay, Admiral. Four hours after the explosion and the fires started, they've still got fires going in a lot of spaces. First they had secondary fires around the uptakes. They started to get a handle on that. Then fires started climbing cable runs and involved decks above the hangar."

"Damn." The admiral said. "We knew that wiring was a problem, but it wasn't considered urgent. Replace it during regularly scheduled overhaul, the Bureau of Ships said."

"I asked Pete if he wasn't about out of things to burn, Admiral. 'Oh, hell yeah, Abner,' he said. 'Aside from 4,675,432 gallons of fuel and God knows how many tons of ammo.'"

"But how are they doing? Are they getting a handle on it?"

"I talked to Smedley. He says the cable runs was the last of the fire jumping to new locations. They paid close attention to those, and he's sure that's isolated. It's just that secondary fires started in a potload of spaces, either from heat through bulkheads or from burning insulation from the cables dropping on bedding and things. It'll take a long time to mop it all up, to make sure none of those areas reflash. Smeds didn't want to say they're turning the corner."

"They still going through supplies like crazy?"

"Yes, sir. Smedley says the helo supply is keeping up, but they use it as fast as it's unloaded."

"Casualties?"

"Nobody killed, Admiral." Abner considered adding "yet" but squelched it. "No new cases. According to Chaplain Dawson, all the kids at the hospital are doing okay. Dawson also said Pete's wife and the *Marianas* ombudsmen have all been up at the hospital."

"The news aspect of this thing?"

"Chaplain Dawson is working notification of next of kin of the injured. The local news channels all have helicopters in the air. The story has gone national. CNN. Public affairs set up a 1-800 hotline number. We've already fielded phone calls from North Carolina, Wisconsin, and Hawaii. Public Affairs has confirmed to the media that the *Marianas* is fighting a fire and that, so far, there are no injuries other than smoke inhalation."

"Wasn't there a lieutenant with burns to the face and hands?"

"Yes, sir." Abner *tsked* at himself for forgetting Lieutenant Zoll. "He's going to be in the hospital a while, but he'll recover.

Should be fit for duty in a couple of months."

"That was the guy who was going to lead the team into the number one engine room right before it blew. If they'd gotten that team into the space a minute sooner, there'd be six deaths. Pete was lucky again. What the hell was he thinking?"

"I talked to him about it, Admiral. It sounded to both of us like he was sitting on the biggest goddamned FAE bomb in the universe. Smeds told me he talked to Fosdick during a couple of breaks in the action. According to Fosdick, Pete said he had 3,500 lives to think about. If there was a 5 percent chance of getting the safeties tripped against an 85 percent chance of killing the team, the team had to go in."

"Pete said that?"

"According to Smeds, Admiral."

"Would you have done that, made that call?" Abner shrugged. "Would you, Admiral?"

"Nobody can truthfully answer that question until he's in that situation. In the Bible—John, I think—there's the saying about the greatest love you can have for another is to lay down your life for him. It certainly costs you something to lay your own life down for another. But what does it cost a commanding officer to lay some of his peoples' lives down to save more?"

26

CAPTAIN PETE ADLER

PETE STOOD IN FRONT OF his chair watching the helicopters sitting on the deck, rotors turning, disgorging pallets of the three vital commodities. Oxygen canisters, firefighting foam, and flashlight batteries.

For want of a horseshoe nail, a kingdom was lost.

The Boss had the flight deck organized and functioning smoothly, but the guys had been at it for—watch check—five hours. Complacency and fatigue, the newest enemies.

He called the Boss with his concern.

"The Flight Deck Officer is rotating his men off the deck for water and chow, and a break. The three spots idea of yours, Cap'n—"

"Okay, Boss," Pete cut him off. "Good job. Just get your flight deck officer and chiefs aside, even if you have to hold a couple helos off the deck for a couple of minutes. Just tell them to watch out for the troops. These guys have been busting ass and we don't want to hurt anyone else at this stage."

"Aye, Cap'n." "Sir."

Solomon stood beside the chair with a tray holding a sandwich.

Pete frowned and waved his hand.

"Cap'n," Solomon said, "XO told me if you wouldn't eat this on your own, I was to put you on the deck gently, kneel on your chest, and ram the damned sandwich down your throat."

A ¾ inch thick slab of ham steak extended beyond the edges of the bread. Oh, it smelled good. Juices started flowing. Pete swallowed, climbed up onto his chair, took the tray and placed it on the shelf under the window next to the cellular phone, and called to Petty Officer Medina, "Fire log."

He took a bite and read.

Fire Log, page 20

1600: Temperatures in engine rooms two, three, and four above 115 degrees. Installed additional emergency ventilation.

1615: All radio communications lost after electrical power secured because of fires in cable runs. Air Boss operating control tower with battery powered emergency radios. No interruption to flow of supplies from the beach.

1645: Secondary fires below hangar deck 50 percent contained. Firefighting efforts under way on three decks between hangar and flight decks. Power restored to radio central. Normal radio comms reestablished.

1700: Vice Admiral Warren's chief of staff informed CO that Chaplain Dawson, CO's wife, and *Marianas* ombudsmen visited injured at Balboa Naval Hospital. Dawson's staff notified next of kin of the injured. Admiral Warren's public affairs officer handling interface with media.

1730: Secondary fires below hangar deck 80 percent contained. Fires above hangar 20 percent contained.

"Captain," Petty Officer Medina said, "The XO gave me this a few minutes ago. He asked me to show it to you when we got a break in the action."

Pete took the pages of typing.

"The lieutenant was the copilot of the helo that ditched, Captain. There's a statement from the pilot too. XO thought you'd want to read this one."

Transcript of Lieutenant Maurice Littlejohn Interview by Safety Officer

We were coming in to land. Everything routine. Winds good, right down the deck. No sun or glare to deal with. Maybe twenty, thirty feet above the deck. No sweat. Done it a thousand times before, right? Then, *blamo!* It hit the fan. I don't know what the hell happened. All of a sudden the helo is thrown into a big assed right bank. I'm looking down at the flight deck. Then we're heading right for the island, and I know we're gonna crash. I know I'm dead. I see this kid staring at me out of a bridge window. Biggest goddamned eyes—they were brown, by the way—I've seen in man or beast. Then, all I can say is thank Jesus F. Christ our squadron skipper was flying that plane. He got us banked left. We missed the island by a *sphinxton*—what? Oh, a *sphinxton* is the smallest measurement in the universe. It's so small it can't be subdivided. A gazillion *sphinxtons* make one red— yes, sir. Moving on. Anyway the skipper gets the bird flying down the flight deck, but that helo is shaking like a mother. Everything I see is blurry 'cause we're vibrating so bad. We clear the bow, lost ground effect, I guess, because we sank like a rock. The skipper hauled up on the collective, and we really started shaking, but we settled onto the water smooth as a baby's butt. I think I took a breath, the first one in a while. I'm wondering how many lives I used up. One, when the helo kicked over into the big-assed bank. We damned near flew into the island, two. Flying down the flight deck, I thought we'd shake ourselves to pieces and crash in a ball of fire, three. Four, we fell off the end of the bow. Then I'm thinking being alive is just so goddamned cool. I only died four times. But I get this feeling and I look out my window to the rear. Do you know how big

> the bow of an aircraft carrier is when it's about to smash into you? Number five death right there, man. All I can do is watch that goddamned carrier coming at us. I cussed the carrier. I cussed the dickhead captain who obviously was screwing off with tea and crumpets. I cussed God for saving us, getting us safely into the water, and then running over us with a hundred thousand tons of steel. You know, if you work at it, you can get a shitload of cussing into a sphinxton of time. Anyway, then I see that bow start to turn, and I'm thinking, is it really turning? Then I'm thinking, is it turning fast enough? Then I know it's going to miss us. And I breathe again. But then I see the stern swinging at us, and I gotta tell you, I said some things to God at that point that probably got me into the worst part of hell, the part that Dante dude couldn't bring himself to write about. But just when I think the stern is going to kill us, it goes the other way. I'm still worried, though. Do people get nine lives? I couldn't remember how many I used. I'm suspicious as hell by that time too, and I'm looking around for the next ball-buster. That's when the skipper tells me to get my head outta my ass and check on the guys in the back. The admiral's staff guy was okay. Our crewman had been knocked out when he banged his head, probably when we got tossed into the right bank, or when we snapped back the other way. He was waking up by the time the boat got us, which was just before our helo sank. The way we were vibrating, we probably shook every rivet in the bird loose. I'm surprised we floated as long as we did. The last thing I want to say is, God, I didn't mean that stuff I said. Thanks, God, really. I'm going to go to church some time. Uh, you're going to take out the part about the carrier CO being a dickhead, aren't you?

Pete called the XO on the walkie-talkie.

"Tell that helo copilot, Lieutenant Littlejohn, the dickhead carrier CO would like to see him on the bridge."

"He went ashore in one of the empty choppers. He seemed kind of anxious to get out of here after he finished talking to our safety guys."

"Another day then. How're the troops holding up?"

"They're doing okay, Cap'n. We're getting people fed, we're rotating crews fighting fires and manning the engineering spaces. The Boss is taking care of the flight deck. Fireball and me, we're watching everything below. We're doing okay."

"You know that half a pig you sent me for supper?" "Yes, sir."

"If nobody else has eaten the other half, I could."

27

PETTY OFFICER SECOND CLASS SAMANTHA INSKO

SAMANTHA INSKO SHUT OFF HER hose, backed out of the smoke-filled berthing compartment, and dogged the watertight door as her oxygen died. Haze and smoke filled the passageway. No spare OBA canister. She mumbled, "The hell with it," and pulled her mask off. The three men handling the hose had no spares either.

"Air's good enough," she hollered over the racket of ventilation fans.

Sliding her back down against the bulkhead, she flopped onto the deck. They were close to the aft end of the ship and right under the flight deck. Looking aft, dark; forward, the emergency lights hung from the overhead every three or four knee-knockers tinted the haze a weird red-yellow-brown, like sci-fi movies depicted the atmosphere on Mars.

She felt like a wrung-out sponge, no bones, no muscles, no strength left, hungry enough to eat a boondocker, and thirsty. Real thirsty. Apparently, breathing pure oxygen did that to you, dried you out.

It was 2000. She and her team had been fighting fires on the 03 level ever since that chief, Cooper, had come back to the hangar from inspecting the upper levels.

The chief had led her up to the 03 level, showed her how to use an electrician to ensure the cables were de-energized, and how to fight the fires smoldering in the runs.

"Start here, Insko," he'd said. "Work aft until you run out of fire. Can you handle it?"

"Bet your ass, Chief," she'd said, and immediately she regretted the word.

The chief had grinned. "Go get 'em, Tiger." And he smacked her on the butt. She whirled and clenched her fists. "Or is it Tigeress? Tigress, maybe?"

The chief handed his radio to her.

"Fire teams are all on channel five. This button here. It'll take me ten minutes to round up another radio. I'm going to want reports from you every fifteen minutes."

"Aye, Chief," she said, still PO'ed.

"I shouldn'ta smacked your butt," he said, and he gave her a little salute. She hadn't expected an apology and didn't know what to do with it.

"Get it in gear, Insko. Or next time I'll kick it."

They pulled apart smoldering mattresses in a berthing compartment and, using a bolt cutters, pulled burnt and smoldering cables in the first compartment. They moved to the next space.

"Why the hell they put wires with insulation that burns like paper on an aircraft carrier?" one of the guys asked. "Dumb-assed civilians in DC."

Another man on the hose they were dragging replied. "Shit, man, count your blessings. Be thankful they didn't design wires that blow up instead of just burn."

Petty Officer Insko was pleased with the bitching. Once it stopped, she began breaking people off two at a time to get something to eat and drink. Only, none of them came back.

They worked aft, dousing fires in compartment after compartment. Finally, she and the three remaining guys knocked out the fires in the last space. They had run out of fire, which was good. She had nothing left to fight another.

Sitting on the deck, she shrugged her shoulders out of the straps supporting the chest plate of her OBA. Her sweaty T-shirt clung to her. Feeling eyes on her, she looked up. The two guys furthest from her turned their heads away. The one closest, the tall skinny kid, continued to leer.

"Shitbird." Guys like him, sometimes they pissed her off. Other times they just made her tired. "We've been fighting the goddamndest fire all friggin' day, and all you think about is a wet T-shirt contest?"

The guy shrugged. A pimply kid. Taller even than Arnold, probably seventeen or eighteen years old. He wiggled his eyebrows. If he was trying to act like Groucho Marx in those ancient movies, he was failing miserably. Samantha rolled her eyes and pushed herself up.

"Come on, guys. Let's get the hose stowed, and then we'll see if we can find some chow."

"Let's leave it. Who gives a shit?" The wise-ass. There was always one.

"I do, which means you do too. Get off your butts and let's get this done."

As if puppets controlled by ganged strings, the three started standing. The wise-ass groaned.

"I don't even know you guys," Samantha said. "Names?" The one farthest away said, "Simon Olson."

"Frank Myers," the middle one said.

Samantha waited for a moment. "You, wise-ass, got a name?" "Yeah. Dick."

Simon and Norman stifled sniggers. "Last name?" Samantha asked.

Dick squirmed with his back against the bulkhead.

Samantha stepped a little closer. "Last name?" She stared up into his eyes.

"Anderson."

Samantha stepped back. "I'm Petty Officer Insko."

"I'll call you *Melones*." Anderson glanced at the other two men. They kept their eyes on the deck.

Samantha waited until Anderson turned to face her, and then she smiled. “Seaman Olson, Seaman Myers, go get some chow. I’m not sure we’re done fighting this fire, but you best use this opportunity while you can.” She looked up at the tall kid. “This wop, Seaman Recruit Dicka You, will get this hose stowed. Seaman Recruit You, you got any idea how to do it properly?”

Anderson, whose real first name turned out to be Marvin, shook his head.

“Figured as much. Listen up. The hose has to be drained and put back on the rack properly so it comes out clean and fast.”

Samantha turned to watch Olson and Myers step over knee-knockers. She wanted them to be far enough away so they wouldn’t hear. The rest of what she had to say to Anderson was for him. She wanted him to listen to her, not worry about what his buds would think of him being chewed on by a girl.

“So, Anderson, could be a flare-up in the middle of the night back in that berthing space. I’d let you screw the hose up if I knew you’d be the only one killed if the fire kicks off again. That happened, the efficiency of my navy would be improved. Hell, the whole human gene pool’d be improved. But if we do need that hose again, and it doesn’t come out right, we could lose some people who really are worth a shit. So pay the hell attention, Dick You.”

After they got the hose properly flaked onto the bulkhead rack, she followed Seaman Anderson down the tunnel of Mars-scape lighting. He wasn’t a bad kid, really. Once he got the proper direction, he did good work. If he’d just let the sexual crap alone. Another 150 ass-kickings or so, he might begin to show some promise. At knee-knockers, the boy had to not only step over the bottom of the bulkhead opening, he had to duck his head to clear the top. She almost said, “These need to be called head-knockers for you, eh?” But she wasn’t so tired she’d let the word *knockers* escape her mouth, not to Marvin.

The sexual stuff did wear her out more than fighting a big-assed fire all goddamned day—and night. It was never even innuendo, always blatant, always in your face, always demoting her to two boobs and a twat. It was enough to drive a woman to lesbianism, which inspired a thought. Her boyfriend, Arnold, back in Lemoore, when she got back, she'd tell him, "Arnold, I've decided to be a lesbian. Not that I don't love you anymore. I do, like a sister."

She almost laughed out loud, picturing his face when she told him. She'd wait until just that point in the evening when romance had had all it could stand of propriety's reining in.

Ahead of her, Marvin turned right and started down the ladder. In the hangar bay someone would know about chow. Clumping down the ladder, she thought about her decision to join the navy. Basically, she wanted to get away from where she grew up, and the "See the world" part of their slogan appealed. All that meant though was "See bars in different parts of the world." Bars, for the most part, had nothing for her, and neither, anymore, did the navy slogan. But her first four years hadn't been too bad. She'd had nothing better to do a year ago and reenlisted for two years. She could have done four or six, but two had a better feel to it. Until she met Arnold, she entertained notions of signing up for four the next time.

Arnold, her cowboy, worked on a ranch where they raised tomatoes, onions, grapes, lettuce, cantaloupes—*melones*. Despite what they raised, it was a ranch, not that F-word, farm.

Below her, Marvin circled the ladder well to descend the last flight to the hangar.

She thought about what she'd done all afternoon and evening, since she'd gone to the hangar bay.

Jesus, this has been the greatest day of my life!

Samantha Insko had been tested, severely. Petty Officer Insko had measured up, majorly.

For the whole rest of her life, however long it might be, Samantha knew she'd probably never have such an...an opportunity again. The CO of the ship wouldn't look at it that way. For sure he'd get his ass booted. But for PO2 Insko, it was pure, unadulterated opportunity. It showed her some things about herself. In the face of pants-pissing danger, others scratched their asses and said, "Oh, dear, what do we do now?"

She had known what to do. All day long, the men in the teams she led followed her lead.

Shit! Why the hell can't life let you get things figured out and then leave you alone? Arnold wants to get married. I wanted to get married—yesterday. Now, after the best damn day of my life, what the hell am I going to tell him now? Damn. I won't even be able to use the lezzie joke. Damn!

28

CAPTAIN PETE ADLER

SLOUCHED IN HIS CHAIR, DRAGGING-ASS tired, he tried to tell himself there wasn't a sailor aboard who wasn't more tired, but Pete wouldn't listen to the little voice.

They'd stopped the helo flights an hour after sunset.

"Risk versus payoff," Pete told his XO. "If we need the supplies, we'll continue. If we think we have enough, we have to turn them off. Everybody's got to be dog-tired."

Harry had checked with Fireball and with the supply officer. Both agreed the flights could stop. Percentage of fire containment both below and above the hangar deck advanced steadily. As the number of worries in Pete's mind diminished, more and more exhaustion oozed in.

He picked up the phone.

"Fred here, Cap'n. I think we licked it, but we're going to revisit every compartment we had fires in. I don't want to declare victory until we get the mop-up done. I'd like to leave my deputy in charge and go with Commander Smedley and survey the damage. Smeds, by the way has got his staff all in at work. We're going to get a handle on the damage and start planning the repair. Okay with that?"

"Hell yeah, Fireball. That's...that's downright satisfactory. Thanks."

That woke Pete up. He'd been sitting there feeling like a whipped old hound dog, too tired to even woof at a raccoon lifting a leg on his haunch. Fireball. He had to be the best damn engineer in the Pacific Fleet. Hell, he was the best in the universe. Fire wasn't all the way out, and he was figuring out how to fix the ship!

Pete hopped out of the chair. His orderly was at parade rest against the rear bulkhead. "Solomon, strike below and get something to eat, brush your teeth, and come back up here. I want you to sleep in my room behind the pilothouse. I want you close tonight, but I'm not going to let you use my toothbrush."

Solomon saluted and left. He didn't smile. Pete thought the toothbrush bit had been pretty funny.

Marines have no sense of humor.

Pete called the XO for a check on the crew.

"A couple of guys got dehydrated. Quack'll stick an IV in 'em if they need it. I've had a couple of search crews look in all the spaces, to make sure we haven't had anyone pass out or something. Haven't found anybody. Musters haven't shown anybody missing either. We've got plenty of good berthing left. We're getting some people to bed."

"Good. You in a position where you can take over on the bridge for an hour or so?"

"Sure. I'll be up in ten minutes. That do it?"

"Yeah. Good. I want to get a look at how much of our warship we burned away."

Pete called Colleen and told her that the big fires were out but that they weren't declaring victory for another couple of hours. She didn't say anything. Then the pause got long.

"You still there, Colleen?"

"Yes. I was thinking about not crying for two hours, until you declare victory. The heck with it. I'm crying now."

She did. He heard a woman's voice ask Colleen what happened and if Pete was okay. "Yes," Colleen wailed. "The fire's almost out. Everybody's okay."

Then both those women were bawling. It was the goddamndest happiest sound he'd heard in his whole frickle-frackin' life.

* * *

When Pete entered the passageway on the second deck, he remembered Lieutenant Littlejohn's reference to Dante. It sure looked like a place made for condemned souls. Above the escape hatch from number one engine room, a shielded bulb was tied to the remnants of brackets in the overhead that once held electrical cables. The cables were burnt away. The bulb threw off gloom, rather than light. Everywhere was black. Pete rubbed his hand over a bulkhead and soot coated his palm. Under the soot, the paint was charred black. Clean Harry's white tile was completely covered with black debris. A mound of charred black rubber from the cables, like cooled lava, filled a corner by a hatchway for a watertight door.

The escape trunk from number one was open, the round hatch lying there with the dogging mechanism missing. When the vapors exploded and blew open the hatch, the explosion must have ripped off the hatch locking mechanism. How the hell did those guys live through that explosion? And Gronk had been standing right there, right next to the hatch when it blew. *Thanks, JC, you know? Just thanks.*

When he first descended from the hangar bay and entered the passageway, smelling the burnt paint, tile, and rubber was as much an act of taste as of olfactory sensing. He could feel the smell sitting on his tongue. He wondered what lethal substances lived in that heavy air. Some of it might be asbestos.

Not another soul was there, neither looking forward nor aft through the gloom. That part of the ship was dead. And Pete felt dead. He couldn't begin to tote up the cost of what the fire had done to his—what *his* fire had done to the *navy's*—ship. His conscience was rather insistent on that point. Some things were not forgivable. His Pop taught him that lesson a long time ago.

He had seen enough and turned to go back to the ladder leading up. There was a drinking fountain in a small alcove. It was covered with soot. He pressed the button on top of the spigot. A stream of water arced up and splashed onto the catch basin. Debris clogged the drain. A puddle started forming. He bent over and took a sip. He was thirsty and guzzled water like a camel that hadn't been able to spit for a week.

He stood up, wiped his mouth on the back of his reasonably clean wrist, and the jukebox in his head cued up "Cool Water," even though what he drank had been warm.

Cool, clear water.

Buoyed up some, he climbed up to the 03 level and stopped by his cabin. The pictures of the past COs were all ruined. Half lay on the deck, frames broken, pictures burnt or charred. The ones still on the bulkhead were all crinkled from heat and smudged with smoke and soot.

He picked up a photo of the first CO. Most of it had been burnt away. A diagonal slice of head containing an eye remained. The stench of disapproval overwhelmed burnt unpleasant chemical compositions. Pete's shoulders sagged. He looked away from the eye, then back at it again. It was his pop's eye.

29

CAPTAIN ABNER BARTON

Abner dialed. The admiral picked up on the first ring. Abner did it the same way, trying to minimize the disruption to the little lady's beauty sleep.

"Pete just called," Abner said. "They got the fire out. Nobody else hurt."

"That's good, but, Jesus," the admiral said. "They burned ten, twelve hours. This'll dick up the carrier schedule. Damn."

"I just talked to Smeds, Admiral. He and Fosdick surveyed the damage. A lot of stuff to fix, no question, but they figured out what's needed. Basically, every navy and every civilian ship repair organization we can put our hands on, including shanghaiing people from shipyards in San Francisco. Smeds already has his guys working on that. By the time the sun comes up, Smeds says, Fosdick'll have a plan together laying out how to use every bit of help we give them. Biggest job is replacing cables. Fires got up in the overhead cable runs and ran the length of the ship in a couple of places. Phones, electrical, electronic equipment cabling has all been damaged. Smeds said they'll be ready to start pulling the old cables out as soon as the ship ties up tomorrow. Bureau of Ships is sending us a team to help manage the recabling effort. Smeds says new cables start going in before the end of next week."

"We have some fine people working for us, don't we, Abner?"

"Yes, sir. Sometimes the only help they need is for us to get the hell out of their way."

"Yeah, but us shore-duty pukes, we're not always boar tits. Today, yesterday, you helped them a lot with all the stuff you heloed out to them."

"What'll you do with Pete, Admiral?"

"Don't know. I've made entries on both sides of his ledger all day. And what Smeds told you about the cause, most of that was not his fault, except one thing. He looked right at the pipe repair job. That feisty little bastard, probably a good thing he was the CO. But he's ruffled feathers. If he could just eke out a little tact—"

"I've known Pete a long time, Admiral. I always thought he was meant to be in command. But after he made O-6, he started bumping into what he calls bureaucratic bullshit. He kneejerk lashes out at it, instead of taking a moment to see if he is lashing at senior officers' sacred cows."

"You know his wife?"

"Some. Chaplain Dawson said she was great with the sailors at Balboa. Then she organized all six of the *Marianas* ombudsmen to answer phone calls from local dependants and relatives from across the country. Chaplain said we learned a lot yesterday about how to handle a major crisis with heavy news involvement. Colleen Adler did a great job."

"A worthy wife, her value is far beyond pearls."

"Proverbs, right, Admiral? Written by the guy with hundreds of wives and thousands of concubines."

"Actually it's from the last chapter, which is attributed to someone else. Lemuel, and if memory serves, it was advice from his mother."

"Ah."

"Ah, yourself, Abner the cynic. Call the duty officer at Pearl Harbor. Give them an update. Tell them I'm going to call the Pentagon at 0700 East Coast time. I'll give the pineapple yahoos an update when they get to work. And have my driver pick me up at five. I should be off the phone by then."

"See you in the…later this morning, Admiral."

30

COMMANDER HAROLD PENNINGTON III

THE CAPTAIN CAME BACK TO the bridge looking beat.

"It's not so bad, Cap'n," Harry said. "We'll get her back together again. Fireball and Smedley are a lot better than all the king's etcetera."

"Yeah. That's the truth." Pete climbed up onto his chair. "Seeing the escape scuttle, and some of the other damage, well, it just sucked the juice, what little I had left, out of me."

"How about if I have the Quack bring you a medicinal? Might help you grab a little nap."

"No. The crew won't get one, I won't either. This night is not over. There's no naptime tonight. Seeing it, well, it was just a kick in the stomach. Takes your breath away. You sit out a play and get back in the game."

The XO nodded and started below, headed for his room on the second deck. His room on the port side had escaped damage. Most of the fire had spent itself on the other side of the ship.

He was tired. His bones were tired. His hair was tired. A shower and even twenty minutes with his eyes shut would do wonders. He clumped down ladders to the 03 level, one level below the flight deck, and stopped. He'd spent a lot of time looking at what the fire had done on the second and third decks, but he hadn't surveyed the 03 level. Fireball told him they'd taken a hit aft on the 03. He'd take a quick look, a few minutes max.

The admiral's quarters smelled of smoke, but the space looked fine. The captain's large in-port cabin also had escaped damage. Outside Pete's cabin, however, tiles were buckled, paint on the bulkhead was scorched, and the pictures of all the past COs going back twenty-plus years, were scorched or burnt up completely.

Forward of the admiral's and the captain's spaces, there didn't seem to be any damage. Looking aft down the long passageway, he couldn't see far. There was one emergency bulb some thirty feet aft of where he stood. Behind that bulb was haze and smoke and utter darkness. He unhooked the flashlight from his belt, flicked it on, and started aft.

Just beyond the bulb, it began. Half the cables in the racks overhead were burnt. Bulkhead paint was scorched. Three or four inches of water covered the deck. The beam of his flashlight didn't so much shine through the air as it slithered around suspended particulate matter.

A couple of knee-knockers later, the air grew nose-wrinkling pungent and made his eyes water. He stopped, considered going back, going to bed. "Screw it," he said and *splooshed* on.

Way ahead, light flickered. *Reflash?*

He hurried aft. His lungs began to protest against the caustic crap he sucked in. He thought he should stop but kept going.

The light came from a doorway into the aft-most berthing compartment. Inside, he counted eight, nine, ten, eleven people wearing helmets with miner-type lights. They were dragging mattresses from bunks and stacking them against a bulkhead.

"What the hell are you people doing?" the XO demanded.

The XO raised his hand to shield his eyes from the eleven lights, which had simultaneously aimed at him. One light danced toward him.

"We're cleaning out burnt bedding, sir. We'll strip all the racks and then lug it down to the hangar bay. We've got a spot designated to stage this stuff."

"Who the hell're you?"

"I, sir, am Petty Officer Insko."

"The girl!"

"She is one a those. Most people pick up on that." It came from one of the others back in the space.

"Attention on deck, you shitheads," Petty Officer Insko barked. "We got a commander here. Anderson, you stand at attention or I'll kick your ass up around your ears."

She took her helmet off, apparently so she could look at him without shining her helmet light in his face. He was shining his light on her chest, so that it wouldn't be in her eyes, thought better of his aim, and moved the beam to her right shoulder. He hadn't recognized her under the helmet and dirt on her face.

Petty Officer Insko, he remembered seeing her on the hangar bay, so long ago. A real looker, and she was a major hard-ass to boot!

Damn.

"Petty Officer Insko, somebody tell you to do what you're doing?"

"I bumped into one your chiefs at chow this evening. I told him the fires were out up here and asked him if there was anything else I could do to help. The chief came up here with me and told me what to do. I rounded up these volunteer yahoos, and we started work."

The XO shined his light on a stack of five-foot lengths of burnt cable.

"You coulda been electrocuted."

"I started with Chief Cooper this afternoon, XO. He showed me how to handle those cables. Every cable in the overhead is dead."

"Damn, Petty Officer Insko. I don't know what to say."

"How about saying you'll get me two dozen more guys, XO? I'll get this friggin space cleaned up and painted fresh as new by the time we tie up."

Jesus. Those goddamned blue eyes atop the rest of the package—

31

CAPTAIN PETE ADLER

THERE WAS SOMETHING WOMBLIKE ABOUT the dark, silent pilothouse at 0235. Soft red light glowed out of the binnacle, and the disembodied helmsman's face hovered above the wheel. The ship steamed west, the lights of San Diego behind it. In front of the binnacle, Pete made out the head and shoulders of the OOD. Still as a statue, he stared through binoculars at the dark ocean and starry sky.

The sky seemed to be formed of three opaque upsidedown bowls over the earth. Pete rubbed his eyes and looked again. The appearance of the sky as bowls remained. One bowl, the farthest, was black as the sea. Stars defined a middle-distance bowl. The nearest appeared as a congealed, coagulated glow from each of the star-dots.

Pete wasn't sure if his eyes could be trusted. He hopped down from his chair and got a mug of coffee. It smelled good. Sometimes it smelled good but tasted scorched from sitting too long at too high a temperature. It tasted good too. The quartermasters generally kept the pot fresh.

He thought about his orderly. Solomon had not wanted to sleep if the CO was awake.

"I'll call your sergeant. He'll bring six marines. They'll put you gently on the deck. One will kneel on your chest. The other five will put your jammies on you and strap you to the bed."

Solomon hit the sack.

He thought of Colleen and realized how much strength he had drawn from her that day—actually the day before. He'd talked to her several times on that wonderful device, the cellular telephone. He'd gotten so much from those talks but knew he'd given her nothing but burden and cause to worry.

He thought about his crew, maybe not his for long, but still his crew at the moment. He thought of the anonymous screw-off, who wasn't anonymous anymore. Petty Officer Griggs. Motivated to do his job, but disdainful of others not of his pack. The rest of the crew, however. In a tight spot, who else would you want in your corner but those guys?

From the rear of the pilothouse, Pete took in the figures of the watch standers in the dim red light. No one moved, only Pete, back to his chair.

He knew there was a lot of activity below. And it wasn't just guys. The XO had called after he found the Amazon-sailor. Petty Officer Insko. And thank God she wasn't one of those who'd cut off a boob, he said. She had been working in that aft berthing compartment. She'd have the space shipshape by the time the ship tied up, she'd said.

After he found her working, Harry got the department heads together and told them to figure out what was damaged in their departments and what needed to be done to fix it. He wanted at least the 85 percent solution by 0600. He would then combine the department plans into a *Marianas* plan. All the departments needed to do what his Amazon and what Fireball Fred were doing. When we got back into port, he told the department heads, "Cap'n will take the plan to Admiral Warren."

It was amazing how things worked out sometimes. The same time the XO was kicking the department heads' asses into gear, Pete got a call from Abner Barton. Admiral Warren did not want the carrier deployment schedule screwed up.

Despite the disaster, Pete saw the fingerprints of God in the persons and actions of Fireball Fred, Commander Smedley, and the XO—and his Amazon.

There were blessings to count. The navy built carriers to take a licking and keep on ticking. The ship was safe, beat up considerably, but the navy would fix it. He hadn't killed anyone.

He had Colleen and the girls. He had enough, and more than he deserved.

He thought of his father's eye accusing him out of that burned photo of the first CO.

For the first time in his life, he thought maybe he deserved the cyclopean version of the look he'd seen so many times growing up.

32

PETEY

On a Friday, two weeks after the Weasel kicked his pop in the shin, Petey walked home from school with Jimmie Joe Kleinhammer. The Fant boys hadn't caused any trouble since that night at Feldeman's barbershop. The nuns no longer stood guard duty from their porch. Halloween was on Sunday.

They were abeam the nun's house. "I'm going to be a pirate," Jimmie Joe said.

"I'm going to be Buck Rogers," Petey said.

Suddenly, he was shoved from behind and fell into the chain link fence along the side of the cemetery. Petey hit the fence with his shoulder, spun around, and wound up sitting on the sidewalk. As he fell, he dropped his Buck Rogers lunch box. He knew the glass inside the thermos wouldn't survive. He knew.

He sat on his butt. The Weasel Fant stood over him with his scraggly brown hair that looked as if it had never encountered a comb, with the tiny, hard black eyes, with the extra belt dangling from the buckle. His brother wasn't there.

"You'll look stupid, momma's boy. Nobody knows how to make a Buck Rogers costume."

The lunch box concerned Petey. He shook it and heard the glass tinkle. No matter how much he didn't want to, he was going to cry.

"Give me that," the Weasel said, reaching for the lunch box.

Petey didn't know where the impulse came from. He'd never been in a fight before. Sitting on the sidewalk next to the chain link cemetery fence, he jerked the lunch box behind him with his left hand. With his right, he punched the Weasel on the nose. The Weasel stood up and said a few words Petey wouldn't think of uttering anywhere, much less right in front of the nuns' house. Petey stood up, eyes on Buck Rogers on top of the tin box.

Suddenly, his head filled with black, then white light. His left ear burned.

"Momma's boy," the Weasel smirked. "Weasel," Petey said through clenched teeth.

The Weasel swung a fist. Petey ducked and then started flailing his arms like a berserk windmill. The Weasel backed away, his arms raised to cover his head.

"Ow," Weasel yelled.

"You boys stop that fighting."

Sister Superior descended the three concrete steps from the covered porch and came at the boys, an avenging angel in black and outrage.

"You come back here, Harry Fant." Sister Superior shouted. The Weasel stopped running for the steps down the hill, turned, and hollered, "Go to hell." To Sister Superior!

Sister Superior was almost as tall as Dick Fant. She taught sixth, seventh, and eighth grades. Next year Pete would encounter Sister Daniels, the middle-grades teacher, and his knuckles would encounter her ruler. Sister Superior didn't use physical punishment, but even in second grade, they—the boys anyway—dreaded sixth grade much more than the ruler.

Sister watched the Weasel until his head disappeared below the edge of the hill. After questioning Jimmie Joe, she sent him home. Then she grabbed Petey's arm, dragged him to the rectory, and confessed his sin to Father Geist.

The boys liked it when Father came to school once a month. He asked about their ball games. The farm boys reported on happenings at their parents' acres. Willie would get going on his pigs and Father always pulled out his pocket watch and pointed to it. Willie would shut up and sit down.

"So, Petey." Father laced his fingers across his potbelly. "What do you have to say for yourself?"

"Harry started it."

Sister stood off to the side of Father's office, her hands up the sleeves. She *tsk, tsked.*

Father pulled open a desk drawer, pulled out a stole, and placed it around his neck.

"I'm going to hear Petey's confession, Sister. You can go back to the convent."

Sister's eyebrows leapt up. "Second graders don't get instruction on confession until after Christmas."

"I'll give him preliminary instruction. Sister Everest can complete his education at the appropriate time," Father said.

Petey swallowed a big lump of trepidation.

Is he expecting me to go to confession right there with him across the desk, looking right at each other? Don't we have to go into one of those boxes at the sides of the rear of church?

Petey glanced at Sister. She stared at Father. Father smiled pleasantly at her. Finally, she spun on her heel and left.

"What's that in your left hand, Pete?"

He looked down at the handle of his lunch box. "Harry ran away, Sister said. Was he bleeding?" "I don't think so, Father."

Father rubbed a hand over his chin. "The sisters teach that it's always wrong to fight, don't they?"

Petey nodded.

"Most of the time, they're right. Some day, if you pay attention to how people behave, if you pray about it, maybe you'll be able to recognize those times when the nuns just may be wrong. Now run along. Otherwise your mother will worry about where you are."

"I don't have to confess, do penance?"

Father smiled. "Sister confessed for you, and you've already done penance. Go along with you now."

"Are you going to tell Momma, or Pop?"

"No. I can't tell anyone about anything I hear during confession. You can't say anything either."

He knew priests couldn't talk about the sins they heard. Father hadn't awarded him any penance, though. According to the older kids, after confessing, they always got a penance, a big or little number of Our Fathers and Hail Marys depending on how bad the sins were. Walking around the church, he wondered about the penance. Then he remembered what Father had said about the nuns maybe being wrong about fighting, which was more puzzling than no penance. The pope was infallible in matters of faith and morals. Infallible meant you couldn't make a mistake. The nuns were infallible about everything.

When Petey got home, his momma told him she had a surprise. Laid out on his bed was a pair of long johns dyed gold. Over the left breast, iron-on letters spelled "Buck Rogers." There was a red ball cap with "Buck Rogers" ironed on it as well. Last Halloween he'd been a baseball player. His momma had bought a gray uniform with knee-high socks. She'd applied "St. Ambrose" to the shirtfront.

He put the ball cap on and held the costume up in front of him. "I'm Buck Rogers."

Momma hugged him and knocked the cap off.

Sunday evening, Petey donned his costume, and Momma took him to the kitchen where Pop was reading the paper.

"Look, Albert," Momma said. "Buck Rogers."

Pop looked around his paper. His head twitched. "Little Petey Pee-pants Adler is not going out of this house in yellow long johns."

Momma looked like she'd been slapped. Petey felt as if he had been. He also felt like crying, but he clamped down on it. He was not going to cry in front of *him*.

His momma was crying. Petey clenched his fists and looked at his pop. The paper was back up.

His momma fled.

For weeks, Petey watched for his pop to make his momma cry again. But he never did. It seemed as if Momma and Pop got along fine, except for that one time. Pop seemed to hate only him.

33

CAPTAIN PETE ADLER

THE PHONE RANG AND KICKED spurs into Pete's heart. He spazzed out of his slouch.

"XO, Cap'n. I'm with Fireball's deputy in DC Central. We have two small reflashes on the third deck, but we can't get any firefighters. They're all working. What do you think? Should we go to GQ and get these things stamped out?"

"Nobody's sleeping, right?" "Probably a few are."

"Two small reflashes? "Third deck, yes, sir."

"Who was that chief pulled you out of the passageway after number one blew?"

"Cooper, sir."

"I got it, XO. No GQ, yet."

"Bosun, blow your pipe for an announcement."

Pete clicked the mic on. "This is the captain. Chief Petty Officer Cooper, I need you to drop what you're doing, form two firefighting teams, go to the third deck starboard side aft. Two reflashes to deal with there. Give me a call on walkie-talkie channel 1. Captain out."

"On the way," came over the talkie.

Five minutes later the chief came back up. "Not a biggie, Cap'n. We're working 'em."

Pete checked his watch: 0330.

The XO and the department heads had developed a plan for

entering port. Tugboats would accompany them all the way in the channel, in case another steering problem arose. They'd tie up at 1000.

Things would start getting busy in the pilothouse as soon as the sun came up though. Commander Smedley had arranged for management personnel from local ship repair organizations to helo to the ship at first light. Not much time left.

Pete went back to the bosun. "Give me the mic back. I'm not done talking."

34

CAPTAIN ABNER BARTON

"I SWEAR TO GOD, CHIEF OF Staff," Commander Smedley said over the cellular telephone, "I never seen nothing like this. Last night, some time after midnight, it's like some spiritual thing infected part of the crew. After fighting the fire all afternoon and evening, they started working on the ship to get it back in fighting shape. And it grew and grew. Pretty soon, everybody was at it. I asked one young kid, probably graduated from high school last year, why he was working so hard. He said, 'Takes more than a pissant fire to kick the Mighty Turkey's ass.' Then he said, 'You mind moving aside, sir?' and he went back to pulling burnt cables out of the overhead. Everybody's calling her the Mighty Turkey now."

"Still nobody else hurt?"

"Right. The XO sent out search teams just to double check. He, Fireball, and me are working on a plan. We've listed all the repairs needed. Fireball right now is working out how to use as much help as we can shanghai to work these repairs. As soon as we tie up, Fireball will be ready to put five hundred men to work."

"The Admiral's worried the *Marianas* fire will screw up the deployment schedule for all the west coast carriers," Abner said. "You think the *Marinas* will be able to deploy on time, the first of December?"

"I asked Captain Adler. He says he won't promise anything yet.

He said he learned a few things about overly rosy forecasts yesterday. He did say that if there was a crew anywhere in the whole universe who could get it done, we should thank God Almighty, because that's exactly who manned and woman-ed the Mighty Turkey."

"That little son of a bitch. He was responsible for getting the crew fired up?"

"I think it was spontaneous, but he was sure part of it. He was on the ship's announcing system several times to give the crew sitreps. He told them, 'Admirals ashore want to know what the hell is going on out here. I figure you got more of a right to know than they do.' The last time he spoke was a couple of hours ago. He told the crew that since 1775, no navy ship ever had a better crew. In the Royal Navy, Nelson never had a better crew. No Roman galley ever had a better crew. 'The Mighty Turkey,' he said, 'is the greatest warship in the universe. That's true because she's got the greatest crew.' Sounds corny when I say it. Sure as hell didn't when he said it.

"He also told them the fire was caused because two people made dumb-assed mistakes, and he was one of the two. He was going to make sure he kicked the ass of the other guy. He told them he knew Admiral Warren would kick his ass and that he had it coming.

"You could hear the crew holler 'No' at the top of their lungs after he said that."

"Where's Pete now?" Abner asked.

"He's over on the starboard side of the pilothouse. He's awarding a Navy Commendation Medal to a female Petty Officer Insko."

"Pete doesn't have the authority to award a Navy Commendation on his own."

"I mentioned that to him. He sent a message out giving the circumstances, stating that he was making the award and that he anticipated expeditious official validation of the medal. To me he said, 'Let the sons-a-bitches try to take it away from her.' Pete's message is probably in your comm center, Chief of Staff."

"What'd she do?"

"She's with the A-7 training squadron and mustered up some of her line crew to help fight the fire. After the fire, she put another crew together, some ship's people, some from her squadron, and they went to work on a burnt-out berthing space. They ripped out all the damaged stuff and are repainting the place right now. She found materials to replace the tiles on the deck. That space will be totally functional by the time we tie up except new cables need to be run through the overhead racks. I wish to hell we had taken a picture of the place when it was all burnt to hell. But they got to work on it before anyone thought of that."

"I guess we better not try to take her medal away from her, then. Is 1000 for tying up to the pier still good?"

"Haven't heard any different, Chief of Staff."

35

CAPTAIN PETE ADLER

When a medal is awarded to a male sailor, it's just pinned on to his shirt. No big deal. Pete had pinned a lot of medals on sailors, but never one on a female. Pinning the medal to Petty Officer Samantha Insko's T-shirt above her left breast was clearly not going to work. Pete knew that before he saw her. He talked to Harry about it.

"Hell, I can't pin it to the back of her shirt. I can't just hand it to her. You put it on her. I'll read the citation."

"That wouldn't be the right way to do it, Cap'n. The award comes from the senior man."

Still-pretty-much-a-mess Clean Harry laughed at Pete behind his weak attempt at a poker face. Pete hissed, probably as much at himself as at laughing-his-ass-off Harry. Pete started self-flogging about what a stupid idea it was to give the bumpy sailor a medal in the first place. But in the second place, the sailor deserved a dad-burned medal, and no amount of technical difficulty diminished that.

"Get a green ribbon. Match the color of the Navy Commendation Medal, if you can handle that, seein's how you're such a worthless piece of trash XO, making your beloved CO think of everything himself."

The ribbon seemed like a great solution, all the way to the time he had Petty Officer Samantha Insko on the starboard side of the pilothouse, still in soiled dungarees, still sooty-faced, and standing at attention as the XO read the citation for the award. Pete began sweating as he thought about how he was going to hang the medal on her. Standing in front of her, the XO's voice droned on about her accomplishments. Pete had to fight his eyes. Her chest exerted a magnetic pull.

Those damned things. Hell, I have five daughters.

But then he wasn't sure if that made it more difficult, not easier.

Clean Harry finished reading. Pete took a breath and went to do his duty.

Petty Officer Insko stared straight ahead as Pete fitted the loop of ribbon over her sweat plastered blond hair and over her ears with his left hand. After lowering the medal to the level of her chin, he dropped it. Her blue eyes jolted Pete.

Pete cleared his throat.

"Normally, Petty Officer Insko, when I give somebody a medal, I say congratulations. I'm saying thanks. The USS *Mighty Turkey*, and all of us in her crew, were lucky to have you as a shipmate these past two days."

Pete saluted her.

"Question, Petty Officer Insko. You still think you'll have the new tile laid this morning?"

"Yes, sir. We'll be done by 1030."

"XO," Pete said. "Push back port entry. I want to tie up at the pier at 1045, and I want to invite Admiral Warren to come and cut the ribbon to the aft berthing space. Petty Officer Insko, I'd like you to present the space to the admiral."

"Sir," she said. "My seabag, all my uniforms were destroyed in the fire."

"The most immaculate set of whites would not be half as proud as the uniform you're wearing right now, Petty Officer Insko. Wear the medal when you present."

"Aye, aye, sir."

The next evolution on that side of the pilothouse was very different. One of a commanding officer's major responsibilities is to maintain good order and discipline. The Uniform Code of Military Justice provides for courts martial and nonjudicial punishment (NJP) to discipline failures of behavior and performance.

Pete and the XO discussed the case of Petty Officer Griggs, a senior first class, married, two children. He had committed crimes: gross dereliction of duty, disobedience of a direct order, and willful disregard of several safety policies and procedures. He recklessly endangered the lives of everyone aboard the *Marianas. He has caused,* Pete thought, *a hundred million dollars in damage, including a lost helicopter.*

He and the XO agreed. There were grounds for a court martial. Courts martial could impose very stiff penalties, including prison time. At NJP, Pete could only reduce a man in rank by one pay grade and fine him. Harry pressed for court martial. But Pete figured he could be fired as soon as the ship tied up. When helicopters started ferrying repair management personnel aboard that morning, he would not have been surprised if Rear Admiral Miller, his boss, had gotten off one of the choppers and relieved him and turned the ship over to Harry. Miller hadn't shown, though. If his time was limited, he wanted to clean up as much of his mess as he could. Griggs certainly qualified as a mess.

Pete sat on his chair. Harry stood next to him.

"On the one hand," Pete said. "One hundred million dollars, and Griggs could have made a lot of widows. He should be punished. On the other hand, the navy needs the Mighty Turkey back in war-fighting shape. A court martial will drag on and on. Officers and men will be tied up testifying."

"A court martial is the thing to do," Harry said.

Pete shook his head. "Getting the Turkey back into war-fighting shape is the thing to do. A court martial will get in the way."

"People are going to question this decision."

"Harry, I think the powers that be have been asking questions about me all day and night. I think they've found their answers. One more question isn't going to make any difference.

Griggs is not escaping punishment. You've seen his face. You put him on suicide watch. I'm doing NJP."

Pete ushered Petty Officer Insko out, and the master-at-arms ushered Griggs in. After running through the NJP script, Pete easily met his criteria to pronounce, "Guilty as charged."

He awarded the max punishment: reduction in rank and a fine of half a month's pay for two months. The second part, the fine, was more a punishment of the man's wife and children. It always bothered Pete when he had to punish a married sailor, but the punishment was still fitting, and supremely merciful compared to what a court martial would have awarded. Then Pete ordered Lance Corporal Solomon to guard Griggs in the CO's cabin until the ship returned to port. Some of the crew might decide to award him their own brand of justice.

Pete called the admiral's chief of staff.

"Okay, Abner. The sun's up on a new day. We're tying up at 1045. We would like to invite Admiral Warren to come aboard and see what the Mighty Turkey has done to start getting back in shape. Can he come?"

"I'm sure he'll want to be there."

"Another thing. The first class petty officer who pumped all the jet fuel and caused the problem, I just held NJP on him. As soon as we're in port, I want to get him off the ship and stashed somewhere. Then I think he should be discharged ASAP."

"People are going to ask why you didn't court martial him." "A court martial would have been appropriate, but I didn't want him hanging around for months while a trial ground along. I thought the crew needed to concentrate on getting the carrier back in war-fighting shape."

Abner didn't respond for a moment. "I'll get our personnel guys working on orders."

"Abner, nobody else on board is at fault for the fire. It was all on Griggs and me. Griggs has been punished, so it's just on me."

"Pete—"

"I'm asking for your help with this, Abner. It's all I'll ever ask you for."

"Come on, Pete. Get your ship back into port. We'll talk about it then."

Pete laid the handset gently in the cellular phone cradle.

He was sure Harry would take over command of the ship sometime soon. When he did, he'd have a thousand things to worry about. With Insko's medal and Grigg's punishment, Harry would be down to 998.

36

PETTY OFFICER SECOND CLASS SAMANTHA INSKO

Petty Officer Insko felt the ship lurch and heard the tugboat toot. She smiled. They made it, with a minute or two to spare.

Three men were fitting the last pieces of Clean-Harry deck tile against the aft bulkhead. Twenty-one of her crew stood, wearing socks, in groups of four or five on the white surface, laughing, *Son-of-a-bitching, I'm-going-to-sleep-for-a-week*-ing.

"Hey," Petty Officer Insko hollered. Even the three tile installers turned to look at her. "We are not done yet. Get those glue buckets out of here. Bag up the extra tile. Stage all the trash in the next compartment forward. And, hopefully, I don't have to remind you, anyone of you dimwits tracks dirt on this white tile's gonna have a choice of which asshole to shit through."

Which started a chorus of hooting. "I just love it when you talk dirty, Petty Officer Insko."

She made sure to smile only on the inside. Those guys would work another twenty-four hours if she told them to. *Good guys. Damn good, at least when the chips were down.*

She stepped out of the berthing area and onto new white tile in the section of passageway just outside the large compartment. She sat on the deck, took a piece of cardboard from a tile box, and started making a sign with a magic marker. When she finished the sign, she masking-taped it to the bulkhead. Forward of that small stretch of resurrected passageway, burnt and blackened surfaces shouted a vivid reminder of the ball-buster fire that had tried its damndest to kill the ship. But in the end, the Mighty Turkey showed how tough she was.

Just beyond her sign, twenty-five pairs of shoes sat on the deck against the bulkhead. A magic-markered piece of masking tape on the toes of the shoes ID'd the owner. Her own petite shoes at the end of the row didn't need tape.

37

COLLEEN

THE CARRIER WAS INCHING TOWARD the quay. Colleen stood next to Admiral Warren, shielded her eyes from the sun, and peered up at the pilothouse windows, trying to find Pete. She could see forms moving about but couldn't determine if one of them was her husband.

"I expected the *Marianas* to show signs of the fire," Colleen said.

The admiral pointed to an area on the side of the carrier under the island. Colleen saw it then, a huge perfect darkened rectangle etched into the light gray paint. Once the admiral pointed it out, it seemed so obvious.

"That's the outer wall of an area called the uptakes, a huge space," Admiral Warren said. "It's where the jet fuel was dumped."

The carrier nudged up against the floats positioned to keep it from crashing into the concrete pier. As the floats compressed, they emitted a human-sounding groan. Along the length of the ship, lines were tossed to sailors on the pier who pulled the forearm-thick ropes to bollards.

"It took so long to put the fire out," Colleen said. "There were times yesterday afternoon I thought the flames would win." "It was a tough one, all right. I'm sure you've heard Pete say that 'It's better to be lucky than good.'" She smiled. "He says it all the time."

"When you're unlucky, you've got to be really good. We were

unlucky with the fuel spill, but fortunate that we had a bunch of really good people on—and do you know, the crew gave her a new name? She is now the USS *Mighty Turkey?*"

"It used to be considered an insult. In the hospital, all the smoke inhalation cases were boys, less than twenty years old, except Lieutenant Zoll. It's hard to imagine boys trapped inside the ship, with such a…an inferno."

"It wasn't only boys. We had a number of female sailors from the F-14 and A-7 training squadrons aboard. A female Petty Officer Insko received a medal for leadership, first, fighting the fire, and then leading a crew to completely restore a damaged berthing space. She is one hell-on-wheels sailor, I'm told. And you, Colleen, I can't thank you enough for visiting the guys at the hospital and working with Chaplain Dawson."

"Admiral." A tall thin lieutenant commander, with the coiled gold loops of an aide on his shoulder, saluted. "The brow's over. We can board now, sir."

The admiral turned and followed his aide toward the gray metal stairs leading to the brow. A queasy feeling roiled in the pit of Colleen's stomach. The admiral hadn't said anything about her husband. She knew he expected to be fired.

Pete had said, "We just moved in. The moving boxes aren't unpacked yet. That's a plus."

The admiral stopped, turned, and gestured for her to come along.

38

COMMANDER HAROLD PENNINGTON III

He led the admiral and his aide up ladders from the hangar bay to the 03 level. Harry mentally kicked himself in the rear. He should have had coveralls handy for them. Both of them were in whites.

When they reached the 03 level, the admiral stopped and turned to his aide.

"Colby, when we get back, round us up some coveralls. We'll need them the next couple of weeks."

"Sorry, Admiral."

The admiral shook his head, exasperated with the boy, Harry thought. "No damn need for you to apologize. It's me who didn't think of it. I've been a shore-duty puke too long." The admiral waved his hand in a "get on with it" command.

Harry led them aft through the now dry passageway, charred paint above and to the sides, burnt, curled tiles underfoot. Ahead, bright light beckoned.

"Jesus," the admiral said.

"Second and third decks are worse, Admiral," Harry said over his shoulder, banged a shin on a knee-knocker, and suppressed the curse.

They hit the newly installed white tile outside the refurbished berthing compartment. In that section of passageway, the bulkheads were freshly painted pale green.

Cables had been stripped from the overhead racks and the overhead was freshly painted too.

"This area looked like those we just came through?" "Just like it, Admiral," Harry said.

"Jesus. The fire was declared out at midnight, right?" "They might have started at 2300..."

Harry saw the cardboard sign taped to the bulkhead and shined his flashlight on it.

TAKE YOUR DAMN SHOES OFF.

"Take this sign down," the XO growled.

From behind Harry, the admiral asked, "Petty Officer Insko, I presume?"

"Yes, sir," she answered from just inside the doorway. "XO," the admiral said. "Take your damn shoes off."

39

CAPTAIN PETE ADLER

After Lance Corporal Solomon escorted freshly demoted PO2 Griggs off the ship, Pete found Colleen on the hangar bay just inboard of the quarterdeck. She looked so clean and fine and pure, he didn't want to touch her. "Silly," she said, hugging him. That hug reminded him of a hymn from church with the line "Would you kiss a leper clean?"

Pete recited the line and said, "I know how a kissed leper feels."

"I am so glad you are home, Pete Adler." She hugged him again. "I know you'll be busy. I just had to put eyes on you."

"You did a major favor for my eyes too." She left and he went back to the pilothouse.

The XO was set to brief the repair plan to Vice Admiral Warren in the battle group commander's spaces amidship on the 03 level. Harry and Fred had done a great job laying out a department-by-department listing of needed repairs. They identified who'd perform each task and had estimated completion dates on a couple of the items.

By lunch, Harry'd probably be acting CO. He was the one to give the brief.

Pete climbed up onto his chair and decided he didn't hate it anymore. He and that chair had come through some things together. It didn't seem possible that it all happened in about twenty-eight hours. Yesterday at that chair, it had been *You've come a long way, baby.* Just then it was more like *You came further than you had any right to expect.* Certainly a lot further than his Pop thought.

"What a difference a day makes" popped into his head.

I need some lighter music.

The phone rang. He snatched it up, but the normal response, "Cap'n," stuck in his throat. It would not come out.

"Pete? You there?" It was Vice Admiral Warren. "Yes, sir."

"Get your ass down here." *Bam.*

Pete clattered down ladders, concentrating fiercely on not stumbling and tumble-assing his way to the bottom. He clenched the muscles of his brain to keep out the black ugliness that pushed to get in: the contemplation of his hanging, and not on the morrow. Outside the door to the battle group commander's spaces, he stopped, took a breath, and entered.

The XO stood between two easels with the briefing materials on them. The admiral, Commander Smedley, Commander Fosdick, and the admiral's aide sat on a row of chairs, watching Pete.

"Who the hell's the CO here?" the admiral demanded, those blue soul-stabbing eyes of his boring into him. "The CO should brief."

Behind Pete, the door from the passageway opened and a sailor barged in. "Captain." Agitation scrunched up the young man's face.

"What's the matter?"

He thrust a piece of paper at Pete, a Red Cross death notification message. Pete had seen a lot of them before, but never one for himself.

Pop died.

Pete expected something to hit him, some kind of emotion, but there was nothing. Not even relief.

"What's that?" The admiral reached out a hand. The admiral read it. "Jesus. Sorry, Pete."

Pete shrugged.

"Harry can brief the recovery plan."

"I'll brief."

"Pete, go on. Take care of your family."

Thoughts fired. *Momma's dead. Pop killed her. I should have—*

He shook his head and stuck his chin out. "I'll brief."

"Pete."

"Who the hell's the CO here, Admiral?"

40

CAPTAIN PETE ADLER

PETE FLIPPED THE LAST PAGE of the brief.

"Admiral, Commanders Smedley and Fosdick laid out the scope of the repair in detail. Smedley's staff worked all night and this morning, and they lined up every available ship-repair man and woman to work on this job. The XO identified the tasks each of the other departments must accomplish to get us ready for sea. We are working all these items as we speak. Questions, sir?"

"Why the hell didn't you give the XO, Fosdick, and Smedley a Meritorious Service Medal? Maybe you only like to pin medals on female sailors."

Pete felt his face get hot as his brain fumbled frantically for something to say. Then they all burst out laughing.

"Colby, go down to the pier and make sure they haven't towed my car away."

Colby hustled away. The admiral stood up, and Pete led him down to the hangar. The after-part of the cavernous bay was bustling. Like wrong-way ants, a row of sailors carted garbage bags of burnt bedding and other charred items to a Dumpster placed on the after aircraft elevator.

The admiral stopped near where he'd met Colleen. "Pete, the schedule is a big deal. If I have to scramble another boat to take the Mighty Turkey's place, it will disrupt all six West Coast carriers, which constitutes screwing with the lives of thirty thousand sailors plus all their dependants. I need to know if you can make deploying on time. It's a big job and tough to scope. I wanted the answer today, but I'll give you until next Wednesday."

A question, desperate to be voiced, bounced up and down on his tongue like a springboard diver: *When are you firing me?* But he kept his mouth shut.

"We'll get you your answer, Admiral."

"Don't pull it out of your ass. I want a date I can count on."

They continued to the quarterdeck. The boatswain mate of the watch called the sideboys to attention. Sailors from the berthing space resurrection crew were arranged in rows forming a corridor for Admiral Warren to pass through to the brow. They were dirty; the admiral, in soot-spotted whites and smudged shoes, relatively immaculate. Petty Officer Insko anchored one row.

The admiral turned to Pete before he started through. "You think our navy is ready for side-*girls*, Pete?"

Pete snapped to attention and saluted, which was the most appropriate answer he could come up with. The boatswain mate blew his pipe. The admiral departed.

Pete ascended the ladders to his inport cabin and hurried past the remaining ruined photos on the bulkhead. He brushed his teeth and felt better, shaved and bettered up another notch. In the shower, the hot water steamed toxins out of his fatigued muscles.

Drying off, he felt an essence of his pop near him. For the first time, though, thinking about his father didn't engender a feeling of threat or fear or shame that he could never measure up to the one man who mattered the most. Everything that happened and no amount of logic applied to the problem ever changed those feelings that rose unbidden out of the belly of his soul.

There was a knock on the door. "Come," Pete hollered.

Lance Corporal Solomon entered. "I turned Petty Officer Griggs over to the base master at arms. They told me they're putting him up in a motel in town."

"Thanks, Lance Corporal. I just got clean, but you and I are going to get dirty. Change in to something more appropriate and report back here in five."

Solomon saluted and was gone.

41

COMMANDER HAROLD PENNINGTON III

HARRY WAS WORRIED ABOUT PETE's boss, Admiral Miller. He and Pete had left messages with Miller's office the day before, during the fire. None of their calls had been returned. Before they entered port, Harry had called and left a message for Miller's chief of staff informing him about the briefing for Admiral Warren. Harry expected Admiral Miller to show up. If he was out of town, the chief of staff should have attended. But nobody from the staff showed up.

Miller's staff, strange bunch.

After Admiral Warren and the others departed, Harry called Rear Admiral Miller's chief of staff in the staff's ashore office and was put through.

"Captain Casper, Harry Pennington here. We just briefed Vice Admiral Warren on our recovery plan." Harry wasn't quite sure how to put the next part and kicked himself for not thinking it all the way through before dialing. Then he decided he was too tired to fart around. "Just wondering why you didn't have anyone here."

"You briefed the vice admiral without clearing it with Admiral Miller?"

"You want us to come over and brief him?" "Admiral Miller will want to talk to Pete." "Right now?"

"No. Tomorrow."

"What time?"

"Admiral's aide will let you know."

The chief of staff hung up and Harry shook his head. It sounded like Captain Casper didn't even know the vice admiral asked for the brief.

Every officer on Miller's staff was a pain in the butt to work with. The chief of staff was worst. In the navy's twelve battle groups, eleven of the commanders were respected aviators who had reputations that penetrated the iron curtain over the Mississippi that kept the East and West Coast navies separated by interplanetary distances. But then there was Miller and his merry band. *Where do we get such men?*—a line from *The Bridges at Toko-Ri*—flitted through the XO's head.

The only thing Casper was worried about was that Pete briefed three-star Admiral Warren without the approval of two-star Admiral Miller.

He went to find Pete to give him the news that more storm clouds were brewing.

Jesus! That's not even news.

42

COLLEEN

COLLEEN SAT AT THE KITCHEN table reading. She heard the car stop in front and she got up to meet Pete at the side door.

He pulled open the screen door, but he just stood there looking at her.

"Come in, silly."

He mounted the steps and the light in the tiny mudroom showed deep dark circles under his eyes. His face looked gray.

In the kitchen the light was better. Pete's circles weren't quite so pronounced. His face wasn't quite so gray.

"Do you need anything to eat?"

"Momma did that, you know? Do you need anything to eat? That was her hello." "Do you?"

"No, thanks. I'm good. My cook's place is operational. Just a little smoke and soot on the bulkheads. I need a squeeze, one and only."

They embraced.

"Oh, you smell good. I wasn't sure if I broke my nose smelling so much smoke and charred aircraft carrier."

"I expected you to smell smoky." "I took four showers today."

"Come on. You should get some sleep."

"Let me sit with you, in our kitchen. I need to just look at you."

They sat across a corner of the table from each other.

Colleen moved her book aside and they held hands. "How are you doing, Pete?"

He glanced down at their joined hands. He squeezed hers and looked up.

"I don't rightly know how to answer that. When I'm busy, it's fine. When I slow down, I feel like I'm running from something and it catches up."

"Your pop?"

"He's the part that seems the strangest. From second grade to when Momma died, I was afraid of him. When she died, I hated him. Today I stopped hating him, and it occurred to me that as much as I think he killed her, I think I could have saved her if I'd just paid attention. I was so caught up in how he didn't like me, saw only disappointment when he looked at me. But all the time I was at home, only once did I hear him say anything mean to her."

"The Buck Rogers costume?"

"Momma was so proud of that get-up. So was I."

"Pete, we've talked about this. You have to put this behind you."

"Well, that time I went home for Aunt Dorothy's funeral. I looked right at the situation, just like I looked at the patch the guys put in the fuel pipe, and I didn't see what should have been plain as day."

"What are you talking about?"

"I told you about how the fire was caused, that last week the guys showed me the patch in the fuel piping that was part of what caused our fire. Until today, until they told me Pop died, I just didn't see that I should have seen what Pop did to Momma too.

"At Aunt Dorothy's funeral, Uncle Pete and everyone else left after the graveside service. Momma and I stayed. She talked about my aunt's diabetes and how it rotted her life away. Both legs amputated, bed sores, blindness. Momma gave her baths twice a week. That day, standing next to Momma, I thought she was sad for Aunt Dorothy and Uncle Pete. Today I realize she was seeing what was ahead for her. She had the disease too, and she wouldn't have Uncle Pete to take care of her. She'd have Pop." "Pete, you can't blame yourself for that. You didn't even know your mother had diabetes at the time."

"Just like at that…stupid fuel pipe. I looked right at Momma and didn't see that something was very, very wrong."

"Pete, you have to be exhausted. Come to bed."

Pete brushed his teeth and got in bed. Colleen took over the bathroom.

When she came out, he was asleep.

He looked so peaceful, all the fear, the worry, even his pop erased.

She got her rosary and knelt beside him. She prayed on a bead and, before the next one, inserted: *He's such a good father to the girls. He tries so hard to be so much more than his father.* She advanced a bead. *He's a good husband, Lord. Every woman should be so lucky as to marry a man who had a rotten father.* Another bead. *The navy is so lucky to have him, Lord. And Lieutenant Zoll.*

That afternoon, she'd gone with Pete to the hospital. All the smoke inhalation cases had been released. Zoll would be there for at least a month. They found him with two IV bottles going, the backs of his hands pink and glistening with ointment. His face was that way too.

Pete stood there looking at his lieutenant and squeezed her hand so hard it hurt. Zoll slowly raised his right hand with the needle inserted into his forearm and taped in place, and he saluted Pete.

Pete popped to attention, returned the salute, and hurried from the room. Colleen squeezed the lieutenant's upper arm and followed Pete. He was standing with his back to the wall.

"Kleenex," he said.

On the ride home he told her that during the fire, the crew inspired him so many times. They'd tackle one problem, and that quick another would pop up. It got Pete down, tired him out. Then someone would do something, like Zoll just did in there.

"I was the CO. It was my job to pump them up."

Her thumb and forefinger pulled another bead forward.

Tomorrow, Lord, Pete has to see Admiral Miller. Miller will convene an inquiry. Please help him bear whatever comes his way.

A spasm shot through Pete's body and scared Colleen. His eyes popped open.

"Colleen. I fell off the world. Sorry, did I kick you out of bed?"

"No, silly."

She got under the sheet, snuggled close to him, and draped her arm over his chest. He sighed once and slept.

She stayed awake and finished her prayers.

III

THE SINS OF THE FATHER

43

CAPTAIN PETE ADLER

COLLEEN DESPISED THE SOUND OF an alarm. Most of the time, she awakened five minutes early to turn it off. Pete loved the thing. He figured the device was there to ensure he got every second of sleep he could.

That morning he punched it off before she did at 0354. He swung his feet out of bed, felt as if he could move a mountain, and thought, *Why would anyone need more than two hours and fifty-four minutes of sleep every other day?*

"Shave; brush your teeth," Colleen whispered, and kissed his elbow, which pretty much obliterated any prospect of further thinking.

He was back in bed at 0357 and a half. Colleen rolled up against him. She sniffed his face.

"Did you get toothpaste in your ears?"

"I thought it would save time if I only used one thing for both jobs. I didn't want to brush my teeth with shaving cream."

Hearing her giggle, he thought his heart would explode.

* * *

Lance Corporal Solomon was scheduled to pick him up at 0500. Pete waited in front of the house. His orderly drove up at 0445.

Usually Pete said, "Burnin' daylight."

That day he got in the front seat with, "Fine marine corps morning, Lance Corporal."

He pulled away from the curb. "Fine navy morning, Cap'n."

Solomon picked up on it. They'd had enough of burning and needed a new morning routine. Great kid, great marine.

Just before the world gets up to go to work again, dark and quiet seem to get extra deep. At times, Pete had found early mornings tingling with threat. That morning, he felt healed, restored, blessed, and infected with the need to sigh contentedly. There'd probably be an inquiry. After the findings were published, Pete was sure he'd be fired. Until that happened, he wasn't going to worry about anything but restoring the *Marianas* to war-fighting shape.

Part of the ship's recovery plan was to hold a repair status meeting every morning at 0600. Pete intended to spend the hour prior visiting parts of the ship that had sustained damage. He wanted to ensure they didn't overlook any problems. He and Solomon had gotten a good start the day before, but during the night, several sealed off spaces were to be opened. The ship was huge, but Pete was determined to visit every nook and cranny.

Solomon had the necessary equipment laid out in Pete's inport cabin. Flashlights, emergency oxygen bottles (deadly or nonbreathable gases sometimes filled rarely accessed compartments), walkie-talkies, and a chipping hammer. Normally, junior sailors wielded the hammers to chip away corrosion prior to painting a metal surface. Pete had started carrying one on his previous ship. If a seaman thought he could get away with it, he'd paint over corrosion or dirt. A chipping hammer exposed such shortcuts.

For the planning meeting, the XO had commandeered a space on the main deck forward of the hangar. He'd fastened whiteboards to the bulkheads all around the compartment. After their exploration, Pete and his orderly arrived at 0555. The room was crowded.

"Attention on deck," Lance Corporal Solomon barked as they entered.

Everyone jumped to their feet with a scraping and bumping of chairs. The civilian workers came to attention too.

"Seats," Pete said, and he marched to the front.

The room was filled with rows of folding metal chairs. Not everyone got a seat. People stood against the bulkheads as well.

The XO sat in the middle of the first row. "You look like shit, Captain."

"Clean Harry, I feel prettier'n I look."

Everybody laughed, and it might have been sincere even though it wasn't all that funny.

"Okay," Pete said. "This, boys and girls, is the War Room. It's for business. No more than twenty-two and a half seconds of frivolity or grab-assing in any four-hour period allowed. I just used up today's allotment. The Air Boss is in charge of this compartment. He will keep the status boards up to date."

Pete pointed to a whiteboard at the front of the compartment. "This is the Help-Needed board. Anybody needs help with supplies, parts, manpower, coordination, whatever, it goes on this board along with time and date the need was identified. This one, next to Help Needed, is Goals."

Yesterday, he wasn't ready to put dates to the plan. Now he was. He wrote:

> GET UNDER WAY FOR TRAINING 1 AUG LIGHT OFF BOILERS IN NUMBER 1 ON 1 NOV DEPLOY TO WEST PACIFIC ON 1 DEC (ON TIME) FULL POWER RUN when Fireball sez

Pete turned around, and Commanders Fosdick and Smedley glanced at each other. Fred shook his head. "I think we should hold off on setting those goals. Admiral Warren said we have till Wednesday."

"Nope, we're not waiting," Pete said. "The battle group and the airwing need to train for the deployment. We have to give them dates to plan to. There they are.

"Next. Commander Smedley, I asked the chief of staff if I could shanghai you. He said I could. Welcome aboard, shipmate. Now, I propose that Fred be responsible for goal one, and you, Commander Smedley, take the second goal. What do you think?"

Fireball turned to the XO. "Skipper, XO, I'm worried about the troops. We could kill someone with these goals."

Pete nodded to the XO.

Harry stood and faced the crowd. "No, we're not going to kill anyone. We are going to work from seven until seven, six days a week. No work on Sundays. We will have civilian ship repair people working nights. We're going to work our asses off, but we are not going to kill any one of us. We work to the plan Commanders Fosdick and Smedley developed. We keep the people on the plan so they don't get in each other's way. You can get a potload of work done in twelve hours if it's intelligently organized and directed. That's what we are counting on from the people in this War Room. If you run into a problem, ask for help. Immediately. Anybody asks for help, the Air Boss will find a solution. If he can't solve the problem in an hour, he calls me or the captain."

The door in the rear of the room opened and a sailor said, "Captain, Admiral Miller wants to see you in his office."

A lot of the sitters turned to look at the intruder. They swiveled back and aimed their eyes at Pete. It was quiet for a couple of seconds.

"Call him back. Tell him I'll be there at seven," he checked his watch, "forty-five."

"Admiral said to tell you when you tried to put it off, he means right now."

"We got it, Cap'n" Harry said.

Pete nodded. "I know you do. One thing I'd like you to discuss, though. How do we status our key teams, such as the people stringing wire, three times a day without interfering with the work? Let me know what you think when I get back."

Which might have been presumptuous.

44

CAPTAIN ABNER BARTON

Usually, Abner had the door to his office open. Knocking, bidding people to enter, those wasted time. Rear Admiral Miller's chief of staff, Captain Gus Casper, walked in and sat in front of Abner's desk.

Abner didn't hide his feelings. He'd been told that any number of times.

Rats, 0637. Nobody ought to have to see Gus before 0700.

Gus, however, was oblivious. And he blathered. The man wouldn't come directly to the point if his youngest daughter's virtue and his own life depended on it. He rambled on about all the things included in a battle group's predeployment training package.

"The main battery of the battle group is the air wing, of course. You being an aviator, Abner, I expect you wouldn't argue with that notion."

"Is there a point, Gus? I'll give you the benefit of the doubt and assume there is. What is it?"

"The fire."

Abner knew, of course. The *Marianas* fire. But he couldn't resist screwing with Gus.

"The *Forrestal, Oriskany, Enterprise*?"

There had been other carrier fires, but Gus, being a surface ship navy guy, probably didn't know about those.

That shut Gus up. He wasn't so oblivious he missed that he was being jacked around.

Abner could see the wheels turning in Gus's head. Gus couldn't vent at the chief of staff of a three-star. It might reflect badly on his two-star boss.

"The *Marianas* fire, Abner. The repairs mean that we have to delay the deployment to enable the airwing and the battle group adequate time to train."

"Admiral Warren says the *Marianas* has to deploy on time." "Impossible."

"Why impossible?"

"Why! Pete Adler burned the shit out of his ship. The whole carrier needs to be rewired. Admiral Miller is convening an investigation into the fire. Pete will be fired."

"The investigation is completed."

"Who did that? That's Admiral Miller's responsibility." "Admiral Warren assigned the investigation to Commander Smedley. The report is complete. Admiral Warren accepted it and forwarded his endorsement to Pearl Harbor and the chief of naval operations. When you get to your office, you should find a copy of the messages in your inbox."

Gus stared, mouth hanging open.

"Well...Admiral Warren...the schedule still needs to slide. Admiral Miller thinks six months."

"*Marianas* deploys on time. First of December. Vice Admiral Warren is getting a tour of the ship and a briefing on how to make the scheduled deployment date at 0700."

Gus frowned.

"I need to use your phone."

"Get your hand off my phone. I'm expecting a call. Use the aide's across the hall."

45

CAPTAIN PETE ADLER

PETE KNOCKED AND ENTERED THE office. Rear Admiral Miller raised his eyes from a folder. Surprise flickered over the admiral's pissed-off expression. Pete was sure his boss had manufactured the angry look just for him.

"What the hell do you think you're doing, showing up here looking like that?"

"I was told you said to come right away, Admiral."

"Not like that for Christ's sake!" He waved a hand. "You just crawl out of a Dumpster?"

Pete stood at attention but kept his eyes locked onto the admiral's.

"You trying to stare me down?"

Pete wasn't, but he didn't intend to appear to cower in front of him either.

The admiral got up and came around the desk. Athletic-looking man, six one, short blond hairspray-plastered- to-his-skull hair, manly-looking jaw and chin, he reminded Pete of the actor Jeff Chandler. He glared down at Pete. Pete glared up. "You spent a lot of time on the phone with Admiral Warren on the fifth. Why didn't you call me?"

"I did call you, Admiral. And I left the cellular telephone number with your office. You never called back."

"Captains call admirals."

"In the middle of big-assed ship fires, captains call admirals who can help."

Pete knew he should have kept his mouth shut. But he expected to be fired, and although he wanted time to resurrect the Mighty Turkey, taking a bunch of crap from a pompous, paper-pushing, bureaucratic, mental—and moral-midget was too much to ask.

The admiral went back around his desk. He sat and smiled. Miller wanted him to sweat. Pete's armpits did.

"I'm convening a board of inquiry at 1300, in flag quarters on the *Marianas*. Have all your officers assembled in the wardroom. I will send word when I want to talk to each of them."

"No."

"What do you mean, *no*?"

"I have every man and woman, enlisted and officer, engaged in getting the ship back in combat shape. I am not stopping so you can hold some pissant inquiry."

"Pissant inquiry? We'll start with admiral's mast on you, 1300. The charge is insubordination."

"I refuse mast. I demand a court martial." "You can't do that."

"You have a legal officer. Ask him, Admiral."

The office door jerked opened. A navy second-class petty officer stuck his head in.

"What the hell, Osmond?" Admiral Miller snarled.

"Admiral Warren called, sir. He's waiting on the quarterdeck of the *Marianas*. He wants two things." Osmond held up a finger. "He wants a tour of the ship." Second finger flipped up. "He wants to know how you are going to train the battle group to deploy on time."

Then Pete smiled. "You want some help with those two things, Admiral?"

46

CAPTAIN ABNER BARTON

Gus Casper walked in the door and Abner groaned. Two visits in one day, and at 1745.

Not many people liked Rear Admiral Miller's chief of staff, Captain Gus Casper. The guys on Admiral Warren's staff called him Captain Friendly-My-Ass, which had quickly been shortened to FMA.

In one way, the two chiefs of staff were alike. They'd both come out of command assignments with middle-of-the-pack fitness reports. *But that is the only goddamned way we're similar,* Abner told himself frequently.

Gus was surface navy, the most form-over-substance branch, at least in the minds of submariners and aviators. Abner knew, understood, and agreed with how he was rated. When an officer screened for command, he counted among the elite. Being selected for subsequent commands meant moving into ever more rarified air. Abner compared himself to his friend Pete quite often. Pete had wound up in challenging situations with each command he'd held, and he'd measured up. That's how he'd come to be selected for command of an aircraft carrier. That's why when the carrier caught fire, Abner was glad Pete was CO and not himself. Abner knew his strengths, and he knew his limitations, just like Dirty Harry said a man should.

Gus, on the other hand, did not seem to be aware he had limitations, although they were glaring and plentiful. He was one of those staff officers who thought he was every bit as much the admiral as the man who actually wore stars. The other thing about Gus, he couldn't come out and say plainly what he wanted. He vocally circumambulated for thirty minutes, departed, and left a man scratching his head and wondering what Gus was really after.

"Admiral Miller intends to reopen the inquiry into the fire," Gus said.

This surprised Abner, and he sat up straight. "Really?" "Tomorrow morning at 0900."

"Has Admiral Miller talked to Vice Admiral Warren?"

"No. He will, after I get back. What Admiral Miller wants to know is how quickly a new CO can be appointed for the *Marianas.* And the admiral wanted me to ask for a new XO also. A clean sweep, so to speak. What do you think? Pull a guy off a carrier that's in a shipyard. Tuesday, Wednesday of next week?"

"Leave my office, Gus," Abner said as he got up and stood behind his desk.

"What?"

"Leave my office." "Why?"

"I'm going to tell Admiral Warren that Admiral Miller doesn't want to deploy on the first of December."

"I never said that."

"Yes, you did. If I were you, Gus, I'd get the hell back to your boss and tell him to expect a call from mine."

"Admiral Miller has gone home for the day."

"You go home too, Gus. It's the last time I tell you nicely." "What are you going to do?"

Abner charged around the desk, grabbed Gus by the arm, jerked him to his feet, backed him out, closed and locked his office, rapped twice on the admiral's door, and entered.

Abner explained what he'd just learned from Captain FMA Casper.

"I could just spit," the admiral said. He shook his head. "I guess

I was too subtle with Miller this morning. Pete and his crew have gotten the repair off to a great start. We are not going to screw with the Mighty Turkey team. New subject. I just got off the phone with Smeds. He said as far as he knew, Pete was not going home for his father's funeral. That true?"

"I've talked to Pete a couple of times today, sir. He didn't mention it. I didn't think to ask."

"What do you know about Pete's father?"

"Nothing, really. Pete was an only child. Grew up in a small farming town in Missouri, not far from St. Louis. That's all I know of his background. He never talked about his father. We never talked about mine, either."

The admiral got up, walked to and looked out the window behind his desk. There wasn't much to see out that window. Stucco walls of other buildings in the compound. A couple of palm trees.

The admiral faced Abner.

"Call Miller. Tell him to get his ass in here and to do it as if his career depended on it. Then get Pete in here. Send in whichever one gets here first."

As Abner left, he wanted to ask about Pete, about keeping his command after the repairs were completed—or even well under way. Abner was on an extension phone taking notes for most of the admiral's official calls. When they discussed the *Marianas* fire, none of the admirals his boss talked to called for Pete's hide to be nailed to the wall. All of those senior officers were concerned with the navy's culpability over the outdated ship's diagrams, which was why Admiral Warren had Smeds do the inquiry. He had not wanted "Miller stomping around in that minefield." Still, Abner didn't know if the admiral could save Pete for very long. Something like the fire generally elicited a knee-jerk bureaucratic "Off with his head."

He also didn't know how Miller screened for a battle group in the first place, or why Warren didn't fire him. If anyone deserved shitcanning, it was that pompous ass, along with his chief of staff and whole damned worthless crew.

A chief of staff was privy to a lot of things, but the inner workings of an admiral's mind held plenty of restricted access closets Abner would never get to peek into.

Abner started dialing Admiral Miller's home number. A big grin bloomed over his face as he waited for someone to answer the phone and inform the big man he had a phone call.

47

CAPTAIN PETE ADLER

PETE HUSTLED OVER TO ADMIRAL Warren's headquarters. He tried to think of a second reason for the summons but came up empty.

The admiral approved the plan to repair the ship. He'd nodded his satisfaction with the proposed steps to train the battle group for deployment. Pete was not needed any more.

Pete felt relief. At least it was over, or would be soon. It wouldn't be hanging over his head any more.

Pete hadn't wanted to enter the navy. His pop pushed him in. It turned out pretty well, though. The navy sent him to college, postgraduate school, flight training, and test pilot school. The *Marianas* was his fourth command. He had Colleen and the girls.

Plenty to be grateful for, not one thing to complain about.

Abner's door was closed. 1825. No surprise. The admiral's aide, a lieutenant commander, sat at a desk marking up a document. Colby Williamson was his name.

"Commander, the admiral wanted to see me."

Colby looked up and smiled. Aides always smiled. You couldn't tell anything from the way they behaved. "He's expecting you, Captain. Go right in."

Pete knocked, entered, and closed the door.

"Why the hell aren't you going home for your father's funeral?"

The admiral sat behind his desk, scowling. Pete struggled to find an answer that wouldn't take all night.

"You have to bury your father. You're going home. That's an order."

The admiral got up from his desk and walked over to where Pete still had a hand on the doorknob.

"Get out of my way. I'm going to my home now." Pete opened his door for him.

Colby jumped to his feet. "Car's waiting for you, Admiral."

48

CAPTAIN PETE ADLER

Colleen's head rested on Pete's shoulder, and she slept with an enviable commitment to the process. Zonked. Pete had a tough time sleeping on an airplane, even a redeye. And he hated just sitting. That Saturday morning, though, it was nice with her asleep against him. Four days prior, he thought he'd never see her again.

Out the window, he marveled, as he always did, at how many lights dotted the southwestern desert below. Driving through in the daytime, it sure didn't look like enough people lived there to warrant that many lights.

During the late seventies, he used redeye flights from LAX to the East Coast frequently. At the time, he had been assigned to a flight test squadron stationed at China Lake, California. Every month, a requirement for a trip to Norfolk, Virginia, or DC would pop up. Redeyes enabled him to spend a day at work in California, travel at night, and arrive on the East Coast for an early morning meeting. On those flights, he brought a briefcase with away-from-home work. Editing other pilots' test reports never failed to knock him out, sometimes for a good hour.

That morning, he didn't have a soporific brief case, but he did have Colleen's soft hair caressing his cheek. The hint of peach from her shampoo made his nose smile. That's how he thought of it. His nose had gotten tired of the smell of burnt aircraft carrier. Her soft, easy breathing imparted restoratives to him as well as to her.

Thanks, God.

He reminded himself to say thank you a little more frequently.

On the *Marianas,* they'd had a good day, especially with the rewiring. Fireball had gotten all the damaged cabling pulled. The ink wasn't even dry on their recovery plan, and they were ahead! Usually, in such an effort, behind was the norm. The crew was amazing. Fireball, Harry, Smedley, they were amazing. They had everything planned down to a gnat's whisker. Labor was not wasted. Nobody got in anyone else's way, almost. The Air Boss was amazing. When a conflict popped up, people asked for help, and he guided them to a solution.

On Monday, stringing new cable would begin. Fireball didn't want to promise, but Pete knew his chief engineer would get the job done with time to spare. Go to sea on the first of August. It was as sure as any promise ever made.

The ship would deploy with Admiral Miller aboard.

No way he'll allow me to remain as the CO of his flagship. No way the navy would want a new CO to take over at the last minute. No way I have more than another week or two as skipper of the Mighty Turkey.

Hopefully, Miller couldn't get rid of him sooner. Pete thought he needed seven days. If he got it, he would infuse the team with enthusiasm, a little more each day. He knew how to do it. All he had to do was to show the people the progress they were making. In the trenches, all a person saw was the endless job in front of his nose. Pete would show them. Momentum would build each day as the enthusiasm grew. The momentum would carry the ship to the first of August and "seaworthy" status.

The air wing and battle group would get their opportunity to train. While they were at sea, below decks in number one, repairs would go on without interfering with operations. But he needed the next week, the Tuesday-to-Saturday part. His pop's funeral was at 1000 on Monday. Colleen and he had a late Monday afternoon flight back to LA. But first the funeral.

After the Red Cross message came, Colleen told him he needed to go home for the funeral.

"He's already buried to me."

Colleen grabbed his chin, which she'd told him tended to jut out when he dug in his heels.

"Stubborn pig-headed German."

The next day, Admiral Warren ordered Pete to bury his pop. He didn't argue with the admiral. There, above the desert, he admitted to the night and the lights dotting the darkness below that he did need to go home. He did need to bury his father.

Loving Colleen was easy, like the song said. She never said, "Told you so."

When they got back to Missouri, he looked forward to visiting his uncle Pete. He hadn't seen him since his aunt Dorothy's funeral. A redeye had carted him home that time too.

That time, standing next to the open grave, after the priest and mourners had left, he and his momma stayed. Pete was convinced now that his momma was seeing her future moving down the same path Dorothy's had. Colleen had been right. Pete didn't know then his momma had diabetes. But he had a second chance to recognize her situation.

A couple of years later, he flew a navy jet home on a "Santa Claus" run. A blivet, an external fuel tank converted to carry baggage, hung from a bomb rack on his aircraft. Pete had the blivet loaded with Christmas presents.

He'd landed at Scott Air Force Base in Illinois. His friend from grade school, Jimmie Joe Kleinhammer, drove an hour to pick him up and bring him to his momma and pop's house.

His pop was at church. He'd begun attending daily Mass and making an evening visitation.

Pete was glad he had a little time with his momma. As the two of them talked about the girls and about Colleen, Pete noticed that the small table next to the stove was filled with pill bottles.

"All those yours?" Pete asked.

"Yes. Takes a lot of those to keep old people going."

"What are they for?" "Blood pressure." "All those for—"

The door opened. His pop came into the house along with a shot of frigid air. The temperature that night had been minus fifteen degrees. His father never said much. Sometimes not even "How do." Sometimes he'd just nod. Still, the man seemed to fill the room with conversation stifling menace. Pop took his seat at the table. Momma dished up his supper. Pete forgot about the pills.

The next morning when he came into the kitchen for breakfast, his pop was at the table. He didn't remember the pills then either. Jimmie Joe ate breakfast with them and then drove Pete back to his airplane.

49

CAPTAIN PETE ADLER

PETE AWOKE. HIS LEFT HIP felt as if a railroad spike had been driven into the joint.

Maybe, God, you can make the seat engineer who designed this sit on it in purgatory for a millennium.

He tried not to disturb Colleen but had to shift weight to his starboard buttock.

"Am I bothering you? Are you able to sleep?" she murmured.

"Don't change a thing for me, not if you care for me," Pete said. "At least you didn't sing it and wake up the other passengers."

She shifted her head a bit and sighed herself back into loose sleep. According to her, *sleep tight* is an invitation to tensed muscles. "Sleep loose" is much more desirable as a nighty-night sendoff.

His recollections roamed back over Aunt Dorothy's funeral, his Christmas visit when he saw the pills and didn't see them.

After the Christmas visit, Pete went back to California, picked up his life and his work. A month later the carrier he was assigned to deployed to the western Pacific. In mid-June, the ship was in the Indian Ocean. An hour before he was to brief for a hop, the mail clerk passed out letters. He had one from his namesake uncle.

Dear Pete,

No easy way to say this. Your momma passed on May 26.

Uncle Pete explained that at 5:30 in the afternoon, Pop wondered why Momma hadn't come to the elevator to drive him home from work. Pop was afflicted with arthritis and shuffled more than walked. The elevator building next to the railroad tracks where Pop worked had no phone, so he hiked to the main office a block away. He called home but got no answer. He could have asked for a ride, but asking for help was the Eighth Deadly Sin. When he finally got home, he found the car in the garage, garage door closed, the motor running, and Momma dead in the driver's seat.

After Pete read the letter, he should have taken himself off the schedule, but he didn't. In his head, he put his momma in a casket, stuck her away in a corner, and he flew. Never before and never after did he ever feel in such intimate communion with an airplane. He felt three loose rivets on the left side of the tail jiggling as the airframe flexed during flight. He sensed the hydraulic fluid, the oil, the fuel coursing through pipes and tubes and the electrons in the wires. It was a training flight, and he was deadly with the practice bombs and invincible in the mock dogfight. For the landing, he received an OK grade, the highest grade, exceedingly rare too. On that flight, he was the best pilot he could, and would, ever be. Of course, if one of his junior officers had gone flying after getting a letter like he did, Pete would have kicked his butt up to his ears. For Pete, flying had been the thing to do.

After he landed, he took the letter to his room and read it again.

The only graveyard in St. Ambrose was the Catholic one. Since Momma had committed suicide, Pop had her buried in a public cemetery in St. Charles. Pop never asked the Red Cross to inform Pete, and it took his uncle a couple of weeks to figure that out and write the letter.

> Pete understood his momma's death as follows:
>
> His momma had seen what the disease did to Aunt Dorothy.

> The number of pill bottles indicated the disease was beginning to defeat his momma's body, just as it had his aunt's.
>
> Debility and being dependent on his pop were not tolerable.
>
> She had taken her life, but his pop had killed his momma just as surely as if he'd shot her.

Then he set his carrier afire. After he'd looked right at the fuel pipe, and if he'd appreciated what he saw, he could have prevented the catastrophe. Then after the Red Cross message came, he realized he had looked at those pill bottles, and if he had just had room in his head for something other than cocooning himself from his pop, he could have saved her life. She could have come to live with them.

50

COLLEEN

COLLEEN STRETCHED HER ARMS OVER her head. Then she rubbed her neck.

"As a pillow, Pete Adler, you could be replaced by a concrete block."

"I love you too."

Colleen got up, used the restroom, and returned to her seat. Pete was setting his watch.

She glanced out the window. It was after five, Midwest time.

The eastern sky was still black, as much as she could see.

"Before your bony shoulder woke me, I was dreaming of your mother. She told me how much she loved you and that she was so proud of you."

"Momma loved you too. You and Aunt Dorothy." "Not like she loved you."

"Sure, I was her son, but remember when you found out I had brothers and sisters I didn't know I had? The second time Momma met you, she told you things she sure never told me. She loved you in a very special way."

Colleen remembered.

She'd been out with Pete four times when she'd been invited to supper with the Adlers. Pete's father had been, well, *aloof* was one way to put it. She had taken to Pete's mother, though. During dinner, and after, while washing dishes, they talked as freely and easily as sisters, or as a niece and an aunt who spoke at niece level.

She sat close to Pete on the drive home.

"Does your mother always do that during dinner, stay on her feet serving you and your father until dessert and coffee are on the table? She never sat down once. She stood off to the side at times like a servant."

"She's always done it that way. My aunt Dorothy puts the food on the table, and then she sits too. My aunt told me once that that's how Momma did it on her father's farm. That's just how she's always done it," Pete said.

The next week Colleen came to supper again to celebrate Pete's seventeenth birthday. When they'd moved to the table, Colleen didn't sit down.

"You sit, Mrs. Adler. I'll serve." Pete's mother was flabbergasted.

"Sit," Colleen said, pulling a chair back for her.

Pete's mother sat and wiped tears with the back of one hand and then with the other.

At the first dinner, Colleen sensed some hurt thing inside the older woman, something carapaced in hardened scar tissue but possessing a spiritual power to inflict pain through physical boundaries.

As Colleen and Mrs. Adler cleaned up after the birthday cake, Pete's mother told her about the three babies she'd lost after she had Pete. Pete and his father had been in the living room watching TV.

After they got on the highway for the drive to Colleen's home, Pete told her that what she'd done for his momma was a wonderful thing.

"Your mother is a very special person."

"You and Momma talked a mile a minute," Pete said as he drove her home. "Obviously she likes you too. What did you talk about?"

"Your brothers and sisters, for one thing." "I don't have any brothers or sisters."

He had two brothers and a sister: George, James, and Mary.

All had been premature and died shortly after birth. "Why wouldn't she tell me that?" Pete asked.

Colleen knew it was a question that didn't want to be answered.

Pete was angry that his mother had confided in her and hadn't told him about his siblings. They drove the rest of the way home in silence. At her front door, his goodnight kiss had been perfunctory. Usually he put enthusiasm into their embrace.

Colleen had gone to sleep that night wondering if Pete would ask her out again. She was beginning to develop fondness for him. If he didn't call, maybe she would ask him to the Sadie Hawkins dance at school in September. Maybe.

The next morning, a Saturday, Pete called and asked her to go with him to visit the graves of his brothers and sister.

They found the small markers together in a spot next to the fence and just above Pete's uncle's house.

"I wish Momma had told me you were here," Pete said looking down at the three small brass plates fixed to the top of dabs of concrete.

"Did you ask her why she didn't tell you?" Colleen asked.

Colleen waited for Pete to answer, and finally she took his hand.

"She said, 'These kinds of things, you just have to deal with them and move on. It was my problem. I didn't want it to be yours.'"

"Losing those babies, I just know it hurt your mother something awful," Colleen said.

"I asked Momma how come she told you and not me," Pete said. "She told me there are some things women talk to each other about but would never say to a man."

What Pete said next surprised Colleen. It was as if he'd ripped his chest open to show her his soul.

He'd told his mother, "Pop thinks I'm a girl. You could have told me."

Colleen thought she saw into the soul of Pete's father, the strange, silent, off-putting man she'd sat across the supper table from twice. In Pete, she saw wounds.

She saw Pete jut out his chin for the first time.

Her heart melted over the hurt in him. At the same time, she was attracted to his strength. She wanted him to take her in his arms.

He did. That's where and when she fell in love with him. She squeezed his arm and laid her head on his boney shoulder.

* * *

Colleen awoke when Pete stirred. They were descending.

51

CAPTAIN PETE ADLER

After Admiral Warren ordered him home, a sense of duty to his progenitor resurrected in Pete. Albert Adler had no other family. Pete's namesake uncle arranged contact with his father's lawyer. Mr. Pastoris wanted to discuss the estate face-to-face.

Pete drove their rental car to his appointment, and Colleen spent the morning with her sister in St. Charles wandering through the shops on Main Street.

Once situated in front of the man's desk, the attorney told Pete that the house was to be sold and all the proceeds from his estate were to be given to Holy Martyrs Catholic Church. Neither Pete nor anyone else was to have anything to do with his estate or the arrangements for his funeral.

"Your father does not want a visitation." Mr. Pastoris sat behind his large dark wooden desk with his fingers interlaced over his paunch. "He wants a funeral Mass, no eulogy, and to be buried in the church cemetery."

"Why couldn't you just tell me this over the phone?" "Delivering news like this," he oozed, "it's my experience face-to-face is better. And since you were coming back…" "You had a great excuse to bill the estate for another hour."

The look on the man's face told Pete it would be more than one hour he billed.

Pete stood. "Just make sure you leave enough for him to buy his way into heaven. Otherwise you'll meet him in the other place. I can tell you from experience, it won't be fun for you."

The lawyer had been talked to that way before. Pete could tell it didn't bother him in the least.

Pete sat in the car for a moment. His seething anger sparked and then fizzled away. For a moment, he felt sorry for Mr. Pastoris, that the man had to grub for money the way he did. Pete shoved thoughts of the lawyer out of his mind. He'd never have to see the man again.

The trip home would bring one good thing. He started the car, drove to his uncle Pete's house, and took him to Denny's for a late breakfast.

Uncle Pete stood five foot ten, weighed 130, but he ate twelve pancakes, one stack with chocolate syrup and whipped cream. His uncle chewed slowly and appeared to concentrate intently on identifying start, middle, and finish flavors in every forkload. Pete finished his omelet and had nothing else to do but watch his uncle trip out on his dining experience. He scraped up the last dribble of chocolate with his finger and licked it off.

"Ah!" He patted his stomach.

Their waitress topped off the mugs. Uncle Pete sipped, winced, blew across the top, and then sipped again cautiously. His face was tanned and wrinkled. He'd worked outside all his life, forty years with the state highway department, and then in his huge garden every day after he retired. The top of his right ear had been removed for a skin cancer. He put his hand up to the elf ear, met Pete's eyes, and smiled.

"I can feel when people look at it," he said. "Oh, don't be embarrassed. It just naturally draws a man's eyes, like 38 Ds."

"Uncle Pete!"

"Well, okay, not like that."

He sat back. "Something you got a right to know now."

His uncle watched a tendril of steam rise over his mug. Pete felt a twinge of anxiety. The way his uncle was behaving, it wasn't a lightweight thing he was about to disclose.

"Spit it out. That's what you always told me."

"Your momma wasn't married when you were conceived." Worry lifted. "I figured that out a long time ago, Uncle Pete."

"Your momma didn't get pregnant by your pop." That took the wind out of his sails.

"Carl Fant," Uncle Pete said.

"I remember Dick and Hank the Weasel Fant from grade school. Who's Carl?"

"Carl was the father of those two boys."

Pete never knew the Fant boys had a father. They had to have had one once. Pete assumed the man had died, or abandoned his family maybe. Nobody talked about it, and it had never occurred to him to ask.

"Wait. Carl Fant's my real father?" "That's not the way to put it." "How the hell should I put it?" Uncle Pete sat back and sipped. "You going to finish the story?"

"You going to make another scene?"

Suddenly, Pete felt exhausted, drained. He shook his head. "Here it is then. When he was a young man, Albert, your pop, moved around the Midwest from one elevator construction job to the next. He was fearless up in the top of those Hicksville skyscrapers. After work, he liked to drink whiskey and fight. He seemed to especially like it when guys would gang up, two, three, even four. He never lost that I heard. Next morning, he never failed to be on the job, way up in the top again."

"Pop?"

"That's how he was."

Pete shook his head. *How could the man Uncle Pete was describing have hidden inside Pop all those years?*

"Carl Fant came from Kansas. He'd never worked an elevator job before, but he did well enough they kept him on. Us town folks didn't know he had a wife and two kids. After work he liked his whiskey too, but not the fighting."

His uncle Pete described a dance at the Volunteer Fire Department truck house. Momma wasn't supposed to go. Her father wanted her to be a nun. She didn't want to be one, but if she had to, she was going to go to one dance before being forced into the convent. Albert was dancing with her when Carl Fant cut in and swung her around the room. The other dancers stopped to watch. Momma's face glowed. The dance was so much better than she had expected. Albert left the dance and walked up the street to Bud's Tavern, had a couple of whiskeys, found nobody to fight with, and went home.

Uncle Pete had helped Momma sneak out. He took her with him and his fiancé, Dorothy, to the dance.

"Clara was having a great time," Uncle Pete said. "I got occupied with Dorothy and realized I hadn't seen your momma for a time. Dorothy and I..."

He stopped talking and hung his head.

Pete was having a hard time accepting what his uncle revealed about his pop. Coming from anyone else, he would have said they were lying. Now, though, he wondered about what was coming about his momma. She was dead, but that didn't stop Pete from worrying about her.

"So what happened? Carl swept her off her feet and she..." "Not like that. Your grandpa never brought soda pop to the house or gave us money for it. Carl kept giving her soda pops, but he'd spiked them. Vodka, I think."

"He raped her?"

Uncle Pete raised his hands. "People looking at us."

"The hell with them. Tell me what happened."

He made Pete promise to quiet down, acknowledged that his momma had been raped, but he refused to say anything more about the dance.

"The next day, I wanted to take after Carl with an ax handle. Clara didn't want me to. She was ashamed, wasn't sure even being a nun would get her to heaven. And she didn't want your grandpa to know."

He turned and looked out the window, then back at Pete. "We kept it from him until she missed her second period.

Then we told your grandma and grandpa. He kicked me out of the house."

"That's why you never visited the farm?"

"He blamed me for sneaking her to the dance."

Pete had always thought Momma, Uncle Pete, and Aunt Dorothy were the three finest people on earth. Nothing his uncle had related changed his mind about that.

"Uncle Pete—"

"The owner of Bud's Tavern told me the next part of the story."

Two months after the dance, several of the elevator workers were in his place. Albert leaned on the bar by himself. Carl Fant and two other guys stood a couple of stools away.

One of Carl Fant's buddies said he heard that the gal Carl had danced with at the firehouse was pregnant. He asked Carl if it was him. Carl said something like, "How the hell would I know."

The buddy said he'd heard the gal was going to be a nun, but now she couldn't. The gal's daddy knew who ruined her. He had a shotgun and was going to wait for Carl at the elevator in the morning. "What you gonna do?" the buddy asked.

Carl said he was gonna haul ass outta town. The buddy asked, "Back to Kansas?" Carl said, "No." The buddy asked, "What about your wife and them two kids?" Carl said, "Not going to Kansas."

Uncle Pete sipped his coffee.

"According to Bud," Uncle Pete said. "Your pop, Albert, told Carl he was trash, and he wanted him to come outside. Albert went out. Carl and his buddies didn't want to go. Bud made them. He didn't want Albert coming back in looking for them.

"Carl grabbed this sawed off bat from behind the bar. One of Carl's buddies had a knife, and the other buddy took a beer bottle and broke it outside. When the guy turned to break his bottle, Albert slugged Carl and took the bat from him. Albert got cut over the ribs with the broken bottle. Your pop hit the beer-bottle guy with the bat. Knocked him out. Carl grabs the knife from his other buddy and stabs your pop in the arm.

Your pop smashed Carl on the head with the bat several times.

Carl died in Bud's parking lot. The beer-bottle guy lived in an institution on Arsenal Street in St. Louis for fifteen years wearing a diaper. Then he died. That other buddy of Carl's ran away."

"Did Pop get in trouble for killing…" Pete rested his elbows on the table and buried his face in his hands.

"It's a load to take in at once," uncle Pete said. "But I ain't done yet."

Pete sat back and dropped his hands on to his lap. He shook his head, slid out of the booth, walked outside, and stood by his rental car. Turning, he saw his uncle sipping coffee. When he'd been inside, Pete couldn't wait to get out of the restarurant. Now he wanted to be back in there.

Inside, he learned that the man who'd been Pop all his life was not his pop, was not Pop. Pete felt as if a major chunk of flesh had been ripped from inside of him. His momma, too. Raped. She wasn't Momma the way she had been. Carl Fant, he was the real Pop.

Who the hell's the real Pete Adler?

"I ain't done yet," uncle Pete had said. Pete reentered the restaurant.

"Coffee's cold," uncle Pete said. "Want a fresh cup?" Pete shook his head. "I'm about to puke."

"Okay. Answer to your question about your pop getting in trouble."

"He's not my pop. Albert. That's his name." "You're mad, but just listen."

Uncle Pete rotated his coffee mug, around and around.

"So, answer to the question. Albert did not get in trouble. Bud and several men from the bar saw the whole fight. Carl and his buddies had a bat, a knife, a busted beer bottle. Albert had his fists, and he came out of it with two stab wounds. Plus most folks, the sheriff, too, I think, figured Carl Fant got the best kind of justice this side of hell."

Uncle Pete put his hand on his nephew's forearm. "Now, you need to listen to this part. You hearing me?"

Pete met his uncle's gaze and nodded.

"The week after Carl died, his wife, Gloria, showed up at the elevator carrying her one-year-old and dragging another older one by the hand. She'd ridden a Greyhound from Salina, Kansas, got out at the highway, and walked the mile to the elevator. She had no money and wanted to know if Carl had some pay coming.

"Long story short," Uncle Pete said. "Albert got the elevator to give him the money Carl had coming, put some of his own with it, and bought Gloria a trailer and stuck it in the woods below Church Hill. He went to Daddy—mine and your momma's father—and said he wanted to marry Clara."

Pete wasn't sure he could breathe. First, church-going teetotaler, Albert, was a whiskey drinking bar brawler. Now, hardnosed Albert, who hated his son, does deeds worthy of canonization?

"Why the hell didn't anybody tell me any of this?"

"Well, Albert had been a tough. After he killed Carl, he got religion, real serious-like. He done right by Gloria Fant, though he didn't need to. He done right by my sister, which he didn't need to."

"You thought he was noble?"

"All of us did. People wondered at first. Was Albert really changed? Would he go back to drinking and fighting? He didn't. He really turned himself around. He was caring for your momma and you. People tried to talk to your…to Albert, but he was never much for that. By the time you turned two or three, it was almost like the Adler family had always been a part of the town, like everybody else. Didn't do anybody any good to talk about it. We put the whole thing behind us."

"Noble!"

Uncle Pete's hand went up to his elf ear.

"Albert wanted one thing from your momma. He wanted children of his own. They all died. Three premature births, and the last one, when you were in fifth grade, I think. She only made it to three months and had bleeding. To save her they had to do a hysterectomy."

Pete had spent a lot of his growing up years wishing someone else could magically be his father.

Shit.

52

COLLEEN

COLLEEN AND HER SISTER KATE sat at a table in the smaller of the two dining rooms in Miss Aimee B's restaurant.

Her sister was blonde, a couple of inches taller, and seven years younger than she was. Mary turned heads. The way she attracted men had seemed to have popped up overnight. Colleen left home and her freckled, ponytailed, beanpole sister to enter nurses' training. When Colleen moved back home, Kate was a freshman in high school. Every school day afternoon, boys were in the living room or around the ping-pong table in the basement. Kate never seemed interested in any one of them. A single boy never came to the house. They came in small packs. Colleen never understood what drew males to her sister. Kate liked to be around them, but she also seemed to have an inviolable personal space, which Colleen considered to be off-putting. Her adulators were not put off, however. Now Kate was a news anchor for a St. Louis TV station. There still was no man in her life, but there were men. As near as Colleen could figure it out, her sister belonged to a group of half a dozen young men and three women, and they did things together. Dating by group.

"I'm sorry," Colleen said. "Pete told me he'd be here by one. You have things to do, you don't have to stay."

"Yes, I do. I can't abandon my sister, and I'm enjoying hearing about the girls. Also, I wanted to talk to Pete about the fire on his aircraft carrier. I wanted to ask him to do an interview."

"I don't think Pete will do that. After the fire, the admiral responsible for West Coast aircraft carriers made it clear that the only navy person interfacing with the press over the *Marianas* fire was the admiral's public affairs officer."

"It won't hurt to ask."

Mary flashed her smile, and Colleen wondered if it would work on Pete.

"Pete was taking his uncle to breakfast. I'll call and see if his uncle is home."

Colleen left the table and was directed to a phone. A few minutes later, she returned to her chair.

"His uncle said he told Pete something about his father that upset him."

"What did he tell him?"

"I asked, but he wouldn't tell me. 'Ask Pete,' he said." "Was Pete still there, at his uncle's?"

"No. He left an hour ago, but he turned left out of his uncle's drive and went up the hill to church. The freeway is the other way."

"Let's see if your sailor boy got lost," Mary said.

"What if he had a flat tire or something and will show up here after we've gone?"

"No problem, big sis. The station has given me a cellular phone for my car. I'll leave my number here."

Holy Martyrs Catholic Church was the only clue they had. As they entered the parking lot, Colleen spotted what might be the car Pete rented. Mary parked next to a small white Chevrolet.

"This is the car," Colleen said.

They checked inside the church, but no one was there.

"Let's check the cemetery. Only thing after that is the rectory," Colleen said.

Kate lifted the latch and pushed open the hearse-wide gate in the chain link fence and Colleen followed her through.

"That for Pete's father?" Kate asked.

Her sister pointed to the left, two rows of tombstones from the gate, and next to the fence. There was a mound of dirt covered with a fake grass carpet.

"I imagine so. Funeral on Monday. They wouldn't dig a grave on Sunday."

Colleen looked toward the far side of the cemetery, toward the corner where Pete's siblings were buried. There was too much foliage to see anything.

Kate started unfastening the straps on her heels. "Why don't you wait on the sidewalk?"

"Lead on, big sis."

53

CAPTAIN PETE ADLER

PETE PARKED IN THE HOLY Martyrs church lot. He remembered dropping his uncle off at his house but had no recollection of driving up the hill to get there.

Out the windshield to his left he saw that the rectory was new. The school, the part he'd attended, had almost been swallowed by additions. The yard where Willie Ochsenzeimer tackled Sister Robert was under a new wing of classrooms. The church building was the same as it always had been. The trees and shrubs were not as he remembered. There'd been a huge elm near the place where the sidewalk made a Y, one strip of concrete leading to the side door of the transept, the other to the sacristy. Now, there were no trees on the south side. He'd seen these new things before, but it was almost as if his mind refused to recognize anything other than the way it had been almost forty years prior.

Pete got out and followed the walk to the side door. No one else was inside. He followed the side aisle to the rear and sat in the last pew. Muted light, all that was garish and glaring filtered by the stained glass, occupied the space, cohabiting with weighty silence. The main and side altars, the statues, the stations of the cross, all were the same as he remembered. There was something close to comfort in seeing familiar saints and Jesuses.

The sanctuary light glowed through the red glass.

God's home.

He remembered 1972. The Easter Offensive had them flying missions into North Vietnam again. But there were still restraints. Pete and his buddies didn't know what the country was trying to do in Nam. One thing was clear: they were not trying to win the war. Somehow, America had gotten itself into a war it didn't want to be in, and then it couldn't find a way to get out of it. One of Pete's buddies had said, "Now there's a cause worth dying for."

At night Pete planned the strike missions diligently and thoroughly. The next day he flew and pressed his bombing runs. He was determined to win his piece of the war. That's what he believed in. For a time, it was all he believed in. He no longer believed in his country, nor did he trust in God.

That was 1972.

The red light from the sanctuary lamp seemed like an eye staring at Pete.

He got up and left the church through the main doors and stood on the top step.

The sky was cloudless. Birds tweeted. The smell of fresh mown grass, the buzz of a mower, floated in the air. To his right, he could see along the cemetery fence to Maple Street below the hill and into town. He'd encountered the Fant boys going that way. When he walked with Willie, the nun-tackler, they walked along the other fence.

Pete saw the mound of dirt with the green carpet over it. He entered the cemetery and walked to the grave. Beside the mound was the hole with the rig in place to lower the casket. The headstone was in place too. Reddish marble etched with crosses and Albert Adler Born October 11, 1908.

Albert must have ordered the stone some time ago. Most of the time, a person died and the tombstone was ordered by relatives and put in place weeks later.

Pete didn't want to be there. He didn't know where he wanted to be, just not there. He walked to the back corner of the cemetery above his uncle Pete's house.

A bronze plate fixed to a rectangular dab of concrete marked each grave.

Infant George Adler
1943

Infant James Adler 1944	Infant Mary Adler 1946

Pete sat on the ground in the space above Mary and next to George and leaned back against the fence.

54

COLLEEN

COLLEEN SAW HIM SLUMPED AGAINST the fence. "Pete!"

He started awake. She ran to him and knelt down. "Are you all right? What happened?"

Pete gripped her arms. "I was dreaming. I wasn't ever going to see you again." His eyes glistened.

"What are you doing here?"

Pete seemed dazed. She leaned forward to see if she could smell booze. No booze.

Pete pushed himself up as Kate approached. "How was shopping and lunch, sis?"

"Pete," Colleen said. "What's going on? What's wrong with you?"

Pete turned around. Colleen followed his gaze. The slope on the other side of the fence fell away sharply. It was covered with trees. Through the leaves and branches she could see the roof of a house.

"My uncle's house," Pete said.

He turned around, his shoulders sagged, his chin dropped onto his chest.

Colleen hugged him. He didn't respond. "What did your uncle tell you?" Colleen asked. Pete shook his head.

"Let me help you. Talk to me," Colleen said.

"Let's get him out of the cemetery," Kate said as she took Pete's right arm.

Colleen took the other and they headed for the gate.

"He has got to be exhausted," Colleen said. "This has been a hard week for him. The last night of good sleep he had was Monday. Then he worked all day Friday before we took the redeye back here."

"I can walk," Pete said, and then he stumbled.

The sisters looked at each other and kept their hands on his biceps. Once they got to the sidewalk outside the cemetery fence, Pete walked better.

"Give me the car keys, Pete," Colleen said.

At the car he handed them over, and Colleen opened the passenger door. Pete flopped back onto the seat and fumbled with his seatbelt.

By the time Colleen got around the car, Pete was asleep. She pointed to him.

"Zonked. Get him some serious shuteye. He'll be good as new," Kate said.

"I'm going to drive us back to the motel and get him in bed." "I'll follow you. You might need help."

"You're a good kid, Kate. I don't care what Mother and Father said about you."

Colleen got a raspberry from her sibling.

As she drove out of the parking lot, she glanced at Pete, and she hoped the light-hearted exchange she'd shared with her sister had not been too inappropriate.

There were a lot of stanzas to the navy hymn, but she couldn't recall one that fit the situation Pete was in, whatever it was. Whatever his uncle Pete had told him.

55

COLLEEN

COLLEEN AWOKE AT 0600, AND as she had several times throughout the night, looked over at Pete. Still asleep. She did the math. He'd been asleep for thirteen hours. She'd left the bathroom door cracked open. Enough light spilled through to illuminate Pete's face. Calm, peaceful.

She recalled the time in 1972 he'd told her about. Normally, navy ships spent forty-five days conducting combat operations, and then they'd get seven days of R & R. After the North Vietnamese launched the 1972 Easter Offensive, Pete's carrier operated for seventy. Pete had flown two and three times a day. The last two weeks, his ship operated on the midnight-to-noon schedule. Pete hated midnight to noon. Pilots awoke at 2130 to brief the first go, when the ship's crew was still watching the evening movie. He could never make his body accept the idea of sleeping in the daytime, and he always had to gut his way through it each and every time the ship flew that schedule. That time in '72, after the extended line period finally ended, Pete flew a plane to the Philippines a day before the ship arrived. He and three other pilots got rooms in the BOQ. The setup was two dual-occupancy rooms with a common sitting room and one common bathroom. Pete was the junior man. He got the bathroom last. The plan was to clean up, change, and get something to eat at the O Club, which served excellent food at very low prices. While he waited for his turn in the shower, Pete laid down on the coffee table in the sitting room. He figured even if he fell asleep it would be so uncomfortable he wouldn't sleep long. He slept for fourteen hours. When his roommates left for the club, they called his name, but he didn't respond. When the happy diners returned to the room, Pete was still zonked. They told Pete the next morning, "Wake you up so you can go to sleep? How does that make sense?"

After being in port for a week, Pete's ship returned to the line. Forty-five days later, his carrier arrived in Hong Kong for R & R. Colleen and a number of navy wives flew over to spend the week with their husbands. It was a hard time for Pete. Ten days prior to the arrival in Hong Kong, Pete's roommate had been shot down and captured. Pete had started questioning his faith. She'd done the right thing to help him then. "Listen, Pete Adler, no godless man is going to be the father of my daughters."

She remembered thinking that it was funny. When things got tough, women turned to God. Men seemed to think that if their strength failed them, there was no hope.

There had been other times when Pete had worked insane hours for extended periods and then just crashed. He'd come out of those okay. And he'd never again lost his faith.

Colleen was hungry. Pete would be too. She got up and went into the bathroom. After her shower, she dried off and cracked open the door to check on Pete. He was sitting up in bed. He saw her. She had nothing on. He didn't react.

Colleen pulled on her nightgown, wrapped a towel around her hair, and sat on the bed by him.

"Colleen," he said. He started reaching his hand to touch her cheek but stopped.

"What did your uncle Pete tell you?"

It was like trying to get information from the girls, when they wanted to attend a party that they knew had a 95 percent chance of disapproval. They thought if they inched out minimal responses, the critical bits that would tip the scale to an unequivocal *no* might be avoided. She'd had practice pulling hen's teeth. It took some time.

Her hair dried a tangled mess. A*s if it weren't already a bad hair day,* she thought. Eventually, he told her.

He finished the recitation with, "So Momma, who was going to be a nun, was raped by a scumbag from Kansas. He's my father. He was also the father of the Fant boys who made my life miserable growing up. They are my brothers. Pop, who isn't really my father, killed the scumbag who is."

Pete sat there like the Scarecrow in *Oz*, nothing solid or substantial to him. She had to be careful if she was to help him. She sensed that anything she tried just then would be rebuffed. She had to let him wallow in it for a bit. Pete talked about helping sailors with alcohol problems. "You can't help them unless they admit to themselves they've hit bottom," he said.

Pete was low, but not bottom low.

He'd gotten sleep. That was something.

"Pete," she said. "Get up. You can shave while I do my hair. I'll get dressed while you shower. Then we're going to get something to eat."

They went to a Denny's on Fifth Street. Pete didn't want anything. Colleen ordered an omelet for him. He ate it.

They went to Mass at St. Peter Church. After the services, friends they'd attended high school with stopped them on the patio in front of church. Colleen was happy to talk to them. Beside her, Pete wanted to get away from there. He didn't want to talk to anyone. The situation forced him to, though.

Another small step.

The bottom wasn't a physical thing. It was mental or spiritual. It was when a person decided that he'd go no lower.

Colleen drove them to a Dierbergs Market, where she bought flowers. Then she drove them to the cemetery where his mother was buried.

At the grave she watched for some reaction from him, maybe outrage that his father had banished his mother's remains to reside with heathens in unconsecrated ground, something. But he just stood there.

"Put the flowers there, Pete."

Pete did. They remained there for a time, and when they got back to the car, Colleen headed for the driver's side, stopped, and thought for a moment. Then she handed the car keys to Pete. He drove them to Holy Martyrs. The parking lot was full. The 11:30 Mass was under way. No one was outside the church. From inside, organ music and choir singing filtered through the walls. The singing sounded as if the church were packed with enthusiastic worshipers.

Colleen had bought flowers for George, James, and Mary Adler too. After Pete placed those, Colleen led him to his father's future resting place.

From behind them, the organ and singing cranked up again. "Albert Adler," Pete read the name on the stone. "This morning I half expected to see 'Here lies a noble man' etched there."

"Some of what he did was noble," Colleen said. "And if he hadn't done what he did, you might not be here. Who can say what would have happened?"

"So much of my life I was afraid of him. I was a disappointment to him. I didn't care if he approved. I would have been happy if he just didn't disapprove."

"Look at the stone, Pete. All that's on it is a name and a place for two dates. That's it. That's all we on earth need to be concerned with. Your father lived on earth for eighty years. The rest is up to St. Peter to take care of."

"Yeah, but—"

"Yeah, but nothing, Pete Adler. Today you are exactly the same man you were yesterday. If you saw St. Peter right now, he'd ask you, 'What have you done? What have you failed to do?' The answers to those questions haven't changed."

He looked at her and back at the headstone.

Almost there, but the stubborn German just won't let go.

"Of course, St. P., he asks the spouses of those appearing before him. I'd say, well now, doesn't he have a fine-sounding name, Yer

Holiness, and I'm pleased to tell ye that this one here, he's a fairly close to satisfactory man."

Pete tried to hold it in, but he couldn't. He laughed. Colleen grabbed his arm. She thought he might fall into the hole.

Then she kissed his chin.

56

CAPTAIN PETE ADLER

PETE LEANED BACK IN HIS chair, elbow on the armrest, chin on his hand. He'd had only a couple of short naps in the last thirty hours, but he wasn't tired.

What would the bastards do next?

The pilothouse was dark. Radios were silent. A red light clicked on over the chart table. A quartermaster plotted the ship's 0400 position and flicked the light off.

October 26. The *Marianas* steamed off the coast of Southern California in company with five other ships of Admiral Miller's battle group. The group would return to San Diego late in the afternoon, but first they had to complete the second day of their two-day battle problem.

Out the bridge windows, stern and running lights showed on three destroyers screening the carrier from submarine attack. The destroyers were where they were supposed to be: green and white lights to Pete's left, white lights dead ahead, red and white lights to his right. North-northeast of the carrier, a hundred miles away, two cruisers were positioned to thwart air attack.

The day before, the first of the two-day battle problem, the enemy mounted large-scale enemy air raids and one surface ship attack against the battle group. *Marianas* aircraft represented the main defensive weapons in the group, and the only offensive weapons.

The battle problem required Miller to not only defend his ships from enemy action, but to mount strikes against targets ashore. Stretching the limited number of aircraft to cover the multitude of demands had been the challenge throughout the first day and into the night. The last major air attack came at midnight. Through the early morning hours, additional enemy bombers tried to sneak into missile range at low altitude, but all had been intercepted. No submarines had been located during the first day. Pete worried about the subs. There was one out there.

Harry materialized next to Pete.

Lance Corporal Solomon brought each of them a mug of coffee.

"Good first day, Cap'n," Harry said.

"Yeah, but now the tough got to get going. People will be tired, airplanes will break, but the threat will probably be higher." "Aircraft are holding up pretty well. Six fighters down.

Supply Officer expects the parts at 0800."

"Good, we'll need them later. Right now I think all hell is about to break loose. The bad guys will hit us before the sun comes up. The captain running our antisub campaign seems to know his stuff. The ones working antiair and antisurface, all they do is call for launching planes. They see the immediate threat, but nobody on Miller's staff gets the big picture."

"Resource management," the XO stated. "Defend against a triple threat while attacking shore targets at the same time."

"A stretch for a single carrier, but that's the problem we have to solve."

"Every call you made yesterday was right on, but I know the two captains running the air and surface wars have complained to Miller that you just ignore their requests for aircraft."

"The admiral can override me if he wants. That's what he's here for."

Pete sipped his coffee.

"I'd like to know how the pilots are holding up. Check with the airwing commander, please? Tell him I expect some heavy action soon."

Harry left, and Pete called the Air Boss to check on the flight deck personnel.

"The guys're handling it," the Boss said.

"Good. I think we're about to get hit." "Bat sense tingling?"

"Hyper tingling, plus I think the battle problem observers tip off the bad guys, just so they crank up the challenge. They probably know we have a launch scheduled for five. Bet you a buck they hit us in the next half hour to screw up the launch."

"No bet."

The phone jangled. The XO.

"Airwing Commander says he's managed the situation. No newbies in any of the alerts. He said everybody's gotten enough rest."

"How's the commander? He taking care of himself?"

"I asked him, Cap'n. He invited me to perform an unnatural sex act on myself."

"So, he's okay. Thanks, Harry."

The phone rang. Combat Information Center.

"The antiair commander wants us to launch the four alert birds."

"Do we have actual radar contacts?" "Yes, sir, 450 miles out."

"Bosun, launch the alert airplanes," Pete shouted.

He heard the bosun's announcement ring out in CIC over the phone.

"Can the cruiser get any of them with missiles?" Pete asked. "Yes, sir. One cruiser is right on the threat axis," the combat information officer replied.

On the flight deck, jet engines whined.

"Okay," Pete said, "We have two fighters on station already. We have to stop the bad guys at 200 miles. After we launch, don't turn the alert aircraft over to the antiair commander. He'd put the planes out at 250. Position them at 150 until we see if the cruiser can nail them. We need to worry about an enemy surface ship sneaking into missile range. Tell the admiral's staff what we're doing."

Pete hung up that phone, picked up another.

"Air Boss, scramble four more fighter planes and two tankers into alert status. If you have to rob planes from the 0500 launch, do it. But I need more alerts ASAP."

The phone rang.

"CIC, Captain. A search plane discovered two enemy surface ships, northeast at 175 miles. They can launch a missile at 150."

A catapult fired. The ship shuddered.

"Vector the first two alert fighters against those ships. The second two alerts, go ahead and release them to the antiair commander."

A cat fired. Then another, amplifying the vibration from the first.

CIC called again.

"Positive sub contact to the west-northwest at 100 miles. In missile range, Cap'n."

"Launch countermeasures. Ask the admiral's staff to have the rest of the ships fire chaff rockets too."

The fourth cat shot. The bosun announced, "Heads up.

Chaff rocket launch port side."

Pete ducked his head to save his night vision as the rockets fired and flashed a bright hole into the blackness.

He called the Air Boss. "How soon on the next alert?" "Ten minutes."

"OOD," Pete said. "Turn left. Be careful. Don't let the flight deck tip. We have aircraft moving out there."

The OOD ordered the left turn. "What heading, Cap'n?" "Keep turning. Do a 360. Come to the original heading.

We'll launch the next alerts when you steady up." The phone rang.

"Admiral wants to know what the hell you're doing." Casper, Miller's chief of staff. "Admiral said to tell you to head south and go to flank speed."

"I just deployed chaff. If we run, we lose the shield it gives us. I'm not running. I'm staying behind the chaff."

"The admiral ordered you to head south at flank speed."

"No. You ordered me, and it's wrong. I'm not doing it." "Me ordering you, it's the same as the admiral."

"If he wants to order me south, put him on the phone." Pete counted. Two. Three. Four. Five.

Nobody said anything.

He slammed the phone down.

57

CAPTAIN ABNER BARTON

At 1930, Abner knocked on Admiral Warren's door, opened it, and stood back to let Rear Admiral Miller enter. "Welcome back home, Admiral."

Admirals called each other by first names, generally. Admiral Warren had just dropped a hint that more formality was expected during their meeting. Abner started walking out, but his boss called him back in.

"I wanted to talk to you alone," Admiral Miller said.

"You want to talk to me about Pete Adler. You think Abner is Pete's friend and can't be trusted with confidential conversations. Who I don't trust is you."

Abner did not like Miller, detested the man actually. Still, it seemed improper to sit in as one admiral chewed another out. He'd been ordered, though.

"So, Admiral, what is it you want to discuss about Pete?" "Pete refused a direct order from me at 0420 this morning. I want to court martial him."

The rear admiral in charge of managing and grading the battle problem had spoken to Admiral Warren an hour ealier. Abner hadn't been invited to sit in on that meeting. He wondered if Pete's disobedience to a direct order had been discussed. Maybe Miller finally had Pete.

Throughout the first stage of repairs, through the at sea periods over the last two months, Miller kept trying to replace the commanding officer of his flagship. Admiral Warren, however, appreciated the way the Mighty Turkey team met the difficulties that arose daily and found ways around them. The Turkey was meeting the schedule challenge he threw down for them. He wasn't about to disrupt the team that functioned so well.

"What was the order?"

"I ordered him to head south at flank speed. We had air, surface, and subsurface threats. All north. I wanted to move away from the threat."

"What would have happened if Pete obeyed?" "We'd have moved away from the threat."

"Could you have launched aircraft heading south?" Abner saw that Miller didn't know.

"The winds were wrong, and you only had three engine rooms on the line. With four you could have made enough speed to launch on that course. To survive in your situation, you had to launch planes. The missile cruiser got some enemy air, but not many of them. And only your planes could deal with the enemy surface ships. If Pete had driven south, the battle problem evaluators said you would have been sunk and gotten the lowest grade they've passed out in the last five years. Do you know what grade you did get?"

Miller squirmed on his chair. Abner squirmed on his. A captain shouldn't watch a three-star chew out another admiral as if he were a boot ensign.

"You got the highest grade in the last five years. You understand what I'm saying? You, Admiral Miller, got the highest grade. One man on the *Marianas* knew and understood the strengths and limitations of his ship *and* of *your* battle group. One man knew how to use those strengths and limitations to defeat the threat that faced you." Admiral Warren's voice got soft. "Who was he?"

Miller appeared to be looking for a way to escape.

Admiral Warren jumped to his feet. "Who the hell was he?

Say his goddamned name."

"Pete, Admiral Warren. Pete."

Admiral Warren sat down and glanced at Abner. Abner didn't move.

"Okay, Admiral Miller, a couple of things. First you and Pete are going to deploy together on the first of December. After the deployment, you will retire. You will get a call about that on Monday. If you want to retire with dignity, you will talk with Pete Adler every day, at least once. You will seek his advice and counsel. If you do that, you just may be able to do what I said, retire with dignity. If you don't get over this stupid animosity, I can guarantee you, you will screw something up mightily, since the only other thing you have on your staff is more toadies, sycophants, and ass-kissers than MacArthur had. Understand what I just told you?"

Abner had begun to feel sorry for the man. "Yes, sir. I understand."

"Do you agree with it?"

Miller seemed to deflate. He nodded. Admiral Warren sat back in his chair.

"The second thing, Admiral. The Mighty Turkey is lighting off the boilers in number one machinery space on the first of November. Pete said it would happen. Commander Smedley says they are ready. The next day I'm coming aboard to pin medals on the officers and men and women who played key roles in fighting the fire. There are also awards for the repair effort. As you know, there is no award for Pete. Pete's XO and Commanders Fosdick and Smedley all pushed for him to get one, but Pete was adamant. He said he told the whole crew that he was one of the guys who caused the fire. He could not under any circumstances accept a medal for fighting the fire. But there is something you can do, Admiral. After I finish handing out awards, what if you presented a Meritorious Service Medal to Pete for his performance during the battle problem?"

"Yes, sir. I'll do that."

Miller scooted to the edge of his chair.

"Thanks for coming over, Admiral," Admiral Warren said. Miller bolted out of the room.

Relief swept through Abner. He was glad Miller's ordeal was over.

Admiral Warren picked up a battery-powered tape recorder off the floor and pushed the stop button.

"Abner, take this and write up a transcript of this meeting. Make one copy only. Mark it for my eyes only. Then take the tape, chop it to bits, and burn it."

"Yes, sir. Uh, Pete won't make admiral will he?" "No. No he won't."

Abner knew not to press it. He started to rise. "Sit."

"Abner, you will never tell another living soul about what happened here. If I hear that you did, I will find you, rip your beating heart out of your chest and squeeze it bone dry in front of your eyes before they go dim. Understand?"

"I love it when you talk admiral to me, sir." "Get the transcript done, wise-ass."

58

CAPTAIN PETE ADLER

THE FIVE ADLER GIRLS STOOD in the kitchen arranged in stair-step order. The two oldest rubbed their eyes and yawned. The two youngest sniffled and wiped tears.

Eileen, in the middle, said, "You better not miss my friggle-fracking graduation."

The ship was due back from deployment on the first of June.

Her graduation was the next day. "Yes, ma'am." Pete saluted her. "Girls," Colleen said.

"The Lord watch over you." Jennifer, the oldest, hugged her dad and stepped back.

"The Lord keep you safe." Helen said. Hug, step back. "The Lord bring you home to us." Eileen said.

The two youngest in unison said, "I love you, Daddy."

Pete knelt and hugged them and wiped the tears from under their eyes.

"Off to bed with you now," Colleen said. They started filing out.

"Jennifer."

"I know, Mom. The runts." They watched them go. "Parting is not sweet sorrow." "You say that every time."

"It's true every time." Pete sighed. "But this will be the last one."

"You haven't decided to get out of the navy."

"Not yet. When my tour is up on the Mighty Turkey, I might get one more job. It's likely to be in the Pentagon. I'm not sure I want two years of that grief."

Pete had brought the subject up with Colleen before, but that's all he'd done, acknowledge that the end of his navy career was ahead of them. But his brain could not imagine a life after the navy. And just then, there was the deployment to get through.

Colleen squeezed his hand. They got in the van and Pete drove them to the pier. He parked in the CO spot and looked up at the island and mast.

"A noble ship, the Mighty Turkey." "With a noble captain."

Pete shook his head.

"You're thinking about Albert Adler and Carl Fant. In the olden days, nobility was an inherited thing."

"Huh."

"What?"

"The car that pulled up to the brow. It's Admiral Miller. I wasn't expecting him until 0800. It's strange. Since he gave me the medal a month ago, he's a different person. He's told me he wants to talk at least once a day. I was expecting the whole six-month deployment to be a fight with him. Maybe it won't be. Strange."

"No, not strange. Mysterious."

He waited, but she wouldn't go on. She wanted him to ask. "Okay, how is it mysterious?"

"Why do ye not know then, that that's how the Lord works?

In mysterious ways."

GLOSSARY OF TERMS

CO	Commanding officer: the senior officer assigned to a navy vessel. He (or she, currently) is ultimately responsible for all aspects of the ship's and the crew's performance and well-being. He is addressed as Captain, regardless of his actual rank. In the way of things nautical, "Captain" comes out as "Cap'n" frequently.
OOD	Officer of the deck: responsible for the ship and crew if the commanding officer or executive officer are not immediately available. At sea, the OOD stands his watch in the pilothouse, ashore on the quarterdeck.
Conning officer	The helmsman and engine order telegraph (EOT) operator are trained to respond only to the officer with responsibility for driving the ship. Responsibility for driving, or conning, is passed much like responsibility in a multipiloted aircraft is passed: "You have control." "I have control." On a ship the

	exchange in passing the conn would go something like, "This is Lieutenant Smith; Lieutenant Jones has the conn." "This is Lieutenant Jones. I have the conn." Both the helmsman and EOT operator must acknowledge the change in conning officer.
XO	Executive officer: second in seniority in a command to the CO. He is called XO or Exec.
Other senior officers	After the CO and XO come the heads of departments. Aboard ship they are typically addressed by their abbreviated titles. The operations officer becomes Ops O; the chief engineer, Cheng; the navigation officer, Gator. On an aircraft carrier, the head of the Air Department is the Air Boss, or Boss. He is responsible for the operation of the control tower, catapults, arresting gear, the movement of aircraft on the flight deck, and for the aviation fuel system. The heads of departments have division officers reporting to them. The Air Boss will have, for instance, a flight deck officer, an arresting gear officer, and an aviation fuels officer. The Cheng will have a damage control assistant (DCA) and a main propulsion assistant (MPA).
Enlisted ranks	There are nine enlisted ranks, E-1 through E-9. E-1 through E-3 are seamen. At E-4, a sailor becomes a petty officer, a noncommissioned officer in the other services. An E-4 is a third-class petty officer, or PO3. An E-5 is a second-class

petty officer, PO2. An E-6 is a first-class petty officer, PO1. The top three enlisted ranks are chief petty officers.

Alert aircraft — When threat conditions warrant, and during times when an aircraft carrier is not conducting flight operations, planes will be placed in alert condition. The alert birds are armed, and a pilot will be in the cockpit. After a requirement to launch occurs, the pilot starts his engines, conducts checks, and in less than five minutes, the plane will be airborne to counter the pop-up threat.

Amphib — Amphibious assault vessel. A classification of navy ships dedicated to transporting marines to a military objective, and then moving the marines ashore via boat or helicopter to assault the objective.

Bridge — Pilothouse and bridge are used interchangeably.

Bosun — Boatswain mate. Designation of a general seamanship specialty. They handle mooring lines, the anchors, the ship's boats. On the bridge, bosun is a term for the boatswain mate of the watch, the senior enlisted man on the bridge watch team.

Condition Zebra — Warships are designed with three levels of damage, fumes, and flooding containment. Passageways and entries into many spaces can be sealed with watertight doors or hatches. Material Condition Xray is the lowest level of watertight and damage containment. Most doors and hatches are open to

	afford ease of access during normal peacetime steaming. The highest level of watertight integrity is Condition Zebra. When combat is imminent, the GQ alarm sounds, the crew is given three to five minutes to get to battle stations, and then Material Condition Zebra is set. All watertight doors and hatches are secured at Condition Zebra.
Decks	On an aircraft carrier, the hangar deck is the main deck. Decks below the main deck are numbered 2 (second deck), three (third deck), etc. Above the hangar, decks are called levels and are designated as 01 level (one deck above the hangar), 02 level (two decks above the hangar), etc.
EOT	Engine order telegraph. Located next to the helm. It passes ship speed signals to the engine rooms. The EOT operator and the helmsman respond only to orders from the conning officer.
GQ	General quarters, battle stations.
Island	The structure on the starboard side of an aircraft carrier, rising several levels above the flight deck. The pilothouse and the control tower are two major functions housed in the island.
Mast	Captain's mast, a term for nonjudicial punishment. If a sailor is accused of violating a provision of the Uniform Code of Military Justice ashore and is referred to mast, the accused can refuse mast and demand a court martial. Punishments are more severe at courts

martial, but the rules of evidence pertain. Defense and prosecuting attorneys are appointed. At mast, the commanding officer acts as judge, jury, prosecutor, and defense attorney. Mast is a weighty responsibility. COs take it seriously.

Sitrep Situation report.

www.ingramcontent.com/pod-product-compliance
Lightning Source LLC
Chambersburg PA
CBHW030411310726
48979CB00002B/373

* 9 7 8 1 9 5 5 1 7 7 4 3 6 *